SHUTTERED HEART

Jane was appalled when her fifteen-year-old niece, Deirdre — a sensation on the New York modelling scene — developed a crush on photographer Dominic Slater, as he was known for dating his models and then breaking their hearts. Jane decided to give Dominic a piece of her mind. However, to her dismay, she found that, like her niece, she was utterly charmed by him. But how would Deirdre react when she found that her aunt was a rival for Dominic's affections?

MEG BUCHANAN

SHUTTERED HEART

Complete and Unabridged

LINFORD
Leicester

First published in Great Britain in 1994 by
Robert Hale Limited,
London

First Linford Edition
published October 1995
by arrangement with
Robert Hale Limited,
London

British Library CIP Data

Buchanan, Meg
Shuttered heart.—Large print ed.—
Linford romance library
I. Title II. Series
813.54 [F]

ISBN 0–7089–7778–2

Published by
F. A. Thorpe (Publishing) Ltd.
Anstey, Leicestershire

Set by Words & Graphics Ltd.
Anstey, Leicestershire
Printed and bound in Great Britain by
T. J. Press (Padstow) Ltd., Padstow, Cornwall

To my parents, Eleanor and Len,
for their love and encouragement

1

THE antique clock on the mantel chimed midnight. Chewing her lower lip worriedly, Jane looked up from the book she was reading. Where was Deirdre? She should have been home hours ago.

With her thumb and forefinger, Jane massaged the ache that had begun between her eyes. The big black-and-white puddle of fur at her feet stirred, then caught his mistress's eye and made a sound more like a chirp than a meow.

Jane knew her cat well. "Forget it, Seymour. You've eaten enough for one day. I'm putting you on a diet." Shaking her head at her pet's seemingly sole concerns with sleeping and eating, she got up from the armchair and padded into the tiny kitchen to make herself yet another cup of tea.

She sent a prayer of thanks heavenward when she heard the sound of a key in her apartment door. It was followed by a gleeful, "Jane, I'm home!"

Jane practically stumbled over an outraged Seymour in her haste to get back into the living-room. How dare Deirdre sound so cheerful when she'd been so worried!

But the reprimand about the lateness of the hour died on her lips. Instead her eyes widened in shock.

"Deirdre, what have you done to yourself?"

Standing in the tidy living-room, all slender six feet of her, was her niece, but she was almost unrecognizable. When Deirdre had left the apartment that morning, her face had been shiny and bare of make-up, her long, freshly washed blonde hair had been pulled back in a bouncy ponytail, and despite her height she'd looked like the 15-year-old she was. Now, however, the girl's big blue eyes appeared caked with at least two tablespoons

2

of mascara, her lips were a full scarlet pout, her normally peaches-and-cream complexion was coated with make-up as white and lustreless as last week's sheets, and her hair was looped and coiled into wild surrealistic shapes, held in place by combs that looked like daggers.

Deirdre rushed to explain. "Oh, Jane, don't you *love* it? It's the way *he* had me made up. It was fantastic! He wanted me to look exotic, and tough, and wild. He even had me pretend to smoke a cigarette — you know, one of those long skinny brown ones — and swear out loud! Oh, he's so sensitive. A real artist — "

Jane didn't know what brown cigarettes and swearing had to do with sensitivity, and right now she didn't care. She zeroed in on *he*. "Who?" she yelled.

The girl groaned in exasperation. "Oh, *Aunt* Jane, you're so . . . so . . . "

Jane cringed at the emphasis on *aunt*, which made her think of little old maids using fussy lace doilies and precious tea services. Also at the label her niece had been about to give her — square, or whatever it was kids called dull people like 30-year-old maiden aunts these days.

Jane exhaled wearily and pushed a hand through her unruly thatch of dark, curly hair. Her thoughts swung back to the urgent phone call she'd received about a month earlier — the call that had changed her life, however temporarily. She'd been working late doing an inventory at the little Greenwich Village bookshop she owned and managed when the phone rang. Muttering about customers who called after business hours, she scrambled to the counter and snatched up the receiver.

"Book Nook," she'd snapped.

It wasn't a customer, but Sharon, her married older sister, calling long-distance from Iowa. "Jane, what are you doing there? I tried your apartment," her sister said, unable to keep the

4

disapproval from her voice, "and when no one answered I just knew you were working late *again* at the damn shop. Don't you ever take time off?" At Jane's silence, she'd dropped her harangue and got to the point. She was phoning, she said, to ask Jane an enormous favour. It's Deirdre. Remember I wrote you a few months ago and sent you that clipping from *The Dubuque Chronicle*?

Jane recalled the brief article headed LOVELY LOCAL TEEN SOARS INTO HIGH FASHION. It told how Deirdre Flaherty had been discovered by a scout for a top New York modelling agency when working after school at her father's hardware store. It went on to say she'd already become a modelling sensation locally.

At Jane's puzzled yes, Sharon had rushed on, "Well, Deirdre — oh, excuse me, her *modelling* name's Dee, she tells us — has got it into her head that she wants to model full-time, and not just 'kid stuff' in Dubuque, but in New

York, 'where it's all happening'. She wants to spend the summer there, then quit school the minute she turns sixteen next October and live there permanently. Bill and I are frantic, but Deirdre says she'll go with or without our permission. Oh, Jane, we're fit to be tied!"

In the end Jane had agreed to let her niece stay with her. Ever since their parents' deaths, Sharon, her husband Bill, and Deirdre had been her only family. You don't say no to that . . .

Jane's gaze and thoughts returned to the excited teenager standing before her now. Recognizing the plea for understanding on the girl's face, Jane softened. "Deirdre, you're so late — you should have called. I was worried." She paused a moment, then added, "Um, are you always got up like that for a photography session?"

"No, but this shoot was different! And then I lost track of the time, and the second I was finished in the studio I ran out and grabbed a cab."

"Okay, so tell me about this photographer, er, artist."

A rhapsodic sigh, then, "His name is Dominic Slater — you must have heard of him!"

"No, 'fraid not." Jane wasn't exactly up on who was who in the fashion world.

"Oh, Jane, he's so-o-o cool! I mean, like, totally. He does this real wild stuff, makes me feel like I can do everything in front of a camera, like I can be anybody I want. It's so exciting!" She paused to take a breath. "Anyway, that's why he kept me working so late. The shoot was going so well we just stayed at it."

Deirdre collapsed dramatically onto the armchair. "He's so . . . beautiful!"

Jane felt a real stab of worry. "Deirdre, your mother has entrusted me with your well-being, and . . . " She hesitated, realizing how Victorian her words sounded.

"Oh, Aunt Jane, come *on*. I'm not a child!"

7

"You *are* a child, Deirdre. Fifteen is a child. I'm sorry if I sound strict, but in future you've got to call me if you're going to be late. Or else . . ."

Or else what, Jane didn't know. Fortunately Deirdre didn't ask.

"Okay," the girl mumbled at last, pushing out her full lower lip. "I will. And I guess I'd better tell you I'll be working with Dom a lot in the next week or so, and we might have other late shoots . . ."

Dom?

" . . . because we're doing a bunch of ads for a new wave fashion designer," Deirdre finished, "and it's real heavy duty."

New wave. So that explained the make-up and hair.

Jane asked, "Doesn't this, er, Dom, know you're only fifteen and that sending you home at ungodly hours isn't, well, done?" Thank you, Miss Jean Brodie.

"Oh, it's okay, Jane. Like, tonight, Dom got into my cab with me. Insisted on seeing me home. So, like, no problem."

A 'wild' and 'beautiful' photographer made a lovely innocent look like Dracula's daughter, kept her up half the night and then shared a darkened cab home with her? As Deirdre went in to the bathroom to wash off the gunk and get ready for bed, Jane swallowed the growing lump of fear in her throat. Deirdre was so young, so impressionable. It was up to her, sane practical Jane, to save her from the wolves, and it suddenly seemed that the slathering jaws were in sight.

But wait. Maybe there was nothing at all particularly unusual or worrisome about today's shoot. Maybe those stories of wild parties and fast living attributed to the trendy fashion set were pure fiction.

But when they retired for the night, Deirdre to the pull-out couch in the living-room and Jane to her somewhat lumpy bedroom mattress, Jane wasn't quite so sure. She made one very determined resolve, however.

Tomorrow, this 'so-o-o cool' Dominic Slater was going to get a visit. From a lady who was anything *but* cool.

* * *

Jane hesitated on the stoop of the expensive brownstone in the East Seventies. She pushed her sunglasses up into her hair and with the back of her hand wiped at the perspiration that had beaded on her hot, flushed forehead. She loved living in New York, loved its pulse — there was no other word to describe its life, its many-faceted offerings of places and people — but she had to admit on a day like today, when she was damp with sweat, when the pavement seemed to burn beneath her feet, when the exhaust from cars and buses had nowhere to go, it seemed, but in her face, she would prefer to be anywhere else.

Taking a deep breath and squaring her shoulders, she reached up and

10

grasped the knocker, then banged it firmly against the brass lion head.

No answer. Maybe he was still in bed, sleeping off the sort of late-night carryings-on his set favoured. Jane tried the knocker again. And then again, harder.

Suddenly the door was flung open, and Jane was met by a blast of cool air-conditioned air. But that wasn't what caused her slight gasp. No. It was the sight of the man who filled the doorway.

He was medium height, but incredibly broad-shouldered and powerfully built. He was casually dressed in jeans and a loose, open-necked white shirt, sleeves rolled up to expose muscular forearms.

Apart from a sprouting of dark chest hair, his neck was bare; Jane had fully expected to see a display of gold chains and medallions and was perversely disappointed to see there were none. His straight black hair was combed starkly back from a high forehead, and his face, with eyes as blue as a winter sky — and just as cold — would have been handsome, had it not been frowning so fiercely.

Jane had never felt quite so conscious of her own appearance. Her gathered black cotton skirt and loose-fitting white blouse were sticking to her in the most unbecoming way, and her hair, she knew, was more unruly than ever.

"Yes?" he barked, before she could find her tongue. "If you're selling something — vacuums, encyclopaedias, religion, what have you — forget it." He began to shut the door.

Jane's hand shot out to stop the motion of the door. "No, I'm not selling anything. Are you Dominic Slater?"

At his curt, suspicious nod, she said, "I need to talk to you about Deirdre."

"Deirdre?" He frowned even more fiercely. "Look. I think you must have the wrong guy, lady. I don't know any Deirdre."

Suddenly Jane remembered. "Dee. She goes by the name of Dee."

His face changed. "Ah, Dee. Yes,

yes, lovely girl. Great bones, but I'm afraid I don't have time to discuss her now."

Jane became incensed. "Dee happens to be my niece, and she's only a child. I won't have her exploited by the likes of you!"

Her words seemed to have the desired effect. His eyes narrowed and he said coldly, "Perhaps you'd better come inside. It's a crime to leave the door open and let the heat in, and it's clear you need to be set straight. I can give you a few minutes, but I don't have much time."

Who does? Jane seethed. Her shop assistant, Nancy, hadn't been able to come in this morning, so the Book Nook was closed until Jane got there. Not good.

Ever since her small inheritance had allowed her to open the shop three years earlier, Jane had made reliability her second name. She'd developed a number of regulars, and in recent months sales had picked up considerably. Jane was enormously pleased, and only wished her parents could have been around to see her modest success. They would have been so proud! Yet somehow the bookshop had helped Jane come to terms with their deaths — fatal heart attacks within six months of each other — for in a sense it was a part of them; for they'd left Jane not only a monetary legacy, but a passion for books.

She followed Dominic into a small, tastefully furnished anteroom. How could Deirdre think he was beautiful? Ruggedly handsome might apply, if one felt charitable — which Jane did not. And how could such a . . . a brute be a photographer? And if Deirdre were to be believed, a sensitive, artistic one?

"Well, Miss?"

"Ms Cathcart."

"Well, *Mizz* Cathcart, would you care to tell me your problem? I'm yours for the next five minutes."

He smiled then. And Jane suddenly had a glimmer of what Deirdre had seen. His face was transformed. The deep groove in his forehead vanished, laugh lines fanned out from the corners of his eyes, and his lips parted to reveal even white teeth in a way that could only be described as . . . sensual. Jane was appalled by her thought.

"Mr Slater — "

"Call me Dom."

Damn, why was he trying to put her off balance? And why was he succeeding? "All right. Dom. Deirdre, er, Dee, came home rather late last night, saying you'd kept her here working — "

"I also live here. Upstairs," he said unnecessarily. The fact did nothing to ease Jane's mind. Then it occurred to her that that was exactly what he'd intended. He enjoyed goading her.

"Look," she went on, refusing to take the bait, "I'm sure that late hours are often the case with people like you but — "

"And what kind of people *are* we, Ms Colbert?"

Jane missed a step. "Cathcart. And, uh . . . I'm sorry, I don't mean to sound insulting. It's just that Deirdre's so young. Only fifteen."

"Fifteen? She told me she was eighteen."

"She told me you knew she was fifteen."

"I assure you I did not, and — "

"Oh, for heaven's sake, what I'm talking about doesn't matter if she's fifteen or fifty!"

"And just what *are* you talking about?"

Jane met his eyes briefly, but it was long enough to feel a peculiar little jolt go through her. This was awful. What was wrong with her? Dominic Slater was the kind of man sane women avoided like a plague of locusts. All charm and style, but short on substance and compassion.

She gritted her teeth. "I just want to be sure there's no — " she hesitated, "hanky-panky." A choice she instantly regretted.

"Hanky-panky? Hanky-panky?" He gave a thoroughly unpleasant snort of laughter. "Excuse me, ma'am, but you don't look a day over twenty-five. How is it you talk like someone's grandmother?"

Jane blushed furiously. "Mr Slater, er, Dom, forgive me for sounding so, um, old-fashioned, but I think — "

Whatever Jane thought was rudely cut off by a crash and sudden flurry of activity in the hall. Then a small, harried-looking woman of indeterminate age stuck her head into the room.

"Dom, sorry to interrupt, but Melanie is having one of her fits. She's starting to throw things. You know how she gets when she's kept waiting. She says if we don't start now she won't be accountable for her actions, and neither, quite frankly, will I."

"All right, Joss, be with you in a moment."

Muttering something about a moment being too long and her life too short,

Joss swept from the room.

Dom turned to Jane. "Look, Ms Cuthbert — "

"Cathcart. It's Cathcart."

"Cathcart. God, what a miserable name. You should change it. Especially as it appears you don't have a first name."

Jane saw red. "How dare you! Cathcart is a perfectly respectable name. My parents were — "

"Please, I'm sure your lineage is impeccable. I'm really just trying to determine your first name. Forgive me." He smiled then, and to her mortification, Jane found herself mesmerized by it once again. And when he added softly, "What is your name, the one friends call you?" she felt a peculiar melting sensation in her midsection.

"Jane," she practically whispered.

"Ah, a solid, no-frills name. It suits you . . . Jane."

With an effort, Jane yanked herself back to earth. "Mr, I mean Dom,

I can't let you take advantage of a young — "

"Enough!" His face resumed its usual frown, and Jane wondered if she'd only imagined the smile and her foolish reaction. "We'll have to discuss this at some other time. Is there someplace I can reach you? Have you got a card? I'll call you . . . "

Jane fumbled in her bag for a business card. He snatched it from her fingers and turned to leave, saying, "You can show yourself out, no doubt?" And without so much as waiting for her assurance that, yes, no doubt, she could, he strode from the room, across the hall and into what Jane assumed was the studio.

She stood where she was, her mind busy with methods of torture. Nothing was too good — or too bad — for him. Ms Cuthbert indeed!

Jane used more than the necessary force to allow the front door to renew contact with the frame. The action suited her black mood. For the first time, she found herself really regretting her promise to Sharon, her sister. She'd been afraid her niece would shatter the routines and rituals of her quiet, orderly world.

And yet, what was it exactly she was trying to protect? Most people would consider her life dull. She lived in a rent-controlled, one-bedroom walkup in the East Village, which was comfortable but hardly lavish. She often worked ten or eleven hours a day, six days a week, and she spent most of her evenings with only Seymour for company. When she did go out, it was usually with Fred Anderson.

Fred was an editor at a publishing house; he shared her love of books and could always be counted on for good conversation. Furthermore, he was sweet, undemanding and *safe*. They dated once or twice a week. Nothing special — a glass of wine, light dinner and talk at a cafe. The occasional concert or play.

Her life *was* dull, she supposed.

She remembered Sharon's saying that basically Deirdre was a good kid, stubborn and headstrong at times, maybe a bit boy-crazy " . . . but aren't all girls her age?" She'd also added that she didn't know how her daughter stayed so slim on the chocolate-coated raisins and bran muffins she was always eating, and maybe Jane's healthy cooking would rub off on her . . .

Okay, Jane thought, having her niece around wasn't so bad, after all. In fact, it was sometimes fun . . . but not last evening. And not this morning's confrontation with Dominic Slater.

She boarded a hot, crowded bus and found herself scowling all the way back to the Village.

2

"JANE, look at this. It's you!"

Edna Johnson thrust the lurid-looking paperback novel in front of Jane's face. Edna was a lonely retired widow whose pension allowed her to live in a modest hotel a few blocks away and indulge her passion for torrid historical-romance sagas. A frequent visitor to the Book Nook, she'd been buying up Jane's limited stock of the books ever since Jane had opened her store, and Jane valued her as a customer and friend. But there were times, and Jane suspected this was going to be one of them, that she wished Edna would seek her romantic fix, as the woman was fond of calling it, elsewhere.

With a great sigh, Jane dragged her gaze away from the order forms she was filling in and did as Edna demanded.

Her reluctance stemmed not from the fact that Edna was keeping her from her paperwork, but from the certainty the demand heralded yet another lecture on her love life, or lack thereof, which next to Edna's latest medical problem, was the elderly woman's favourite topic.

Now, with *Love's Savage Passion* in the forefront of her vision, Jane blinked and dutifully examined the cover painting. "I suppose there is a similarity," she acknowledged. "And — "

Suddenly the cover claimed her full attention. But it wasn't the heroine who was responsible, but the hero. For he bore a striking resemblance to Dominic Slater. And the pose of the heroine, that of ecstatic submission, made Jane feel almost ill. It had been three days since her encounter with the photographer, three days during which she had alternately wished him on another planet and then on her doorstep so she could tell him what she thought of him, three days during which she had endured Deirdre's singing his praises . . .

"Jane, what's wrong? You've gone pale, I didn't think the fact that you look like a romantic heroine would upset you. It's just that, well, you hide yourself away in those dark clothes and this dark shop — don't get me wrong, I love this shop — but you're like a cloistered nun. Here you are, so pretty and young — "

"Edna, please! I'm okay, really. Just tired."

" — and the good Lord knows, you need a man like that in your life," Edna finished, not missing a beat. She jabbed a be-ringed finger at the black-haired chunk of machismo on the cover.

Jane pushed aside the image the book had triggered in her mind of Dominic Slater and herself in a passionate embrace. What was the matter with her? It was unthinkable. Ludicrous. "Oh, Edna," she said, laughing, "if the good Lord is watching my love life, He certainly wouldn't approve of a man like that! And I'm not remotely interested in men like that, either."

Which of course was not entirely true, Jane knew, but then, physical attraction was not the sort of thing on which to build a lasting relationship. "Edna, I do date someone."

"You mean Fred? Hardly man enough for you. Oh my, yes, he's very pleasant, and I hear tell he's good at his job, but he's so, oh — " Edna screwed up her face " — dull."

"Edna, you mustn't talk about Fred that way. He's a good man, intelligent. I appreciate him and he appreciates me, and that's import — "

"Appreciates? What about love?"

Jane was saved from further discussion, because a couple of other customers were demanding her attention. As the afternoon wore on, Jane found she was not quite up to her usual efficiency. Her assistant, Nancy, had the day off, so no relief there. She was finding it hard to focus on the business of selling, for her rebellious mind was set squarely on innocent virgins beset by macho, bronzed birds of prey. Although Jane was relatively inexperienced with men compared to most single women her age living in New York, she'd had her share, and she knew how to protect herself from vultures. At least she did now . . .

Her mind drifted back to her earlier days in New York. To Charles Dunlevy, a novelist whose latest book was a runaway bestseller. She'd met him at a book-signing when she'd been in New York only a year and was employed as a junior editor at a book publisher. He'd asked her out to dinner, and that had been the start of a year-long romance.

The affair had been exciting, promising. Jane, an intelligent but naive 24-year-old, had fallen completely for the dashing writer, and he'd appeared equally smitten with her. Appeared, it turned out, was the operative word. While Jane had been full of plans for their glorious future together, he had been busy devising ways to juggle the women in his life.

The day Jane had discovered his duplicity was one that caused her pain even now, almost five years later. It was the Sunday of a weekend when Charles had gone to Philadelphia to conduct some research for his new novel — or so he said. Sunday had been one of those first beautiful spring days, with the promise of warmth and roses and love in the air. Jane, missing Charles and feeling the need to somehow be close to him, had purchased a bunch of flowers from a street vendor. She intended to leave them outside his apartment door with an affectionate note to greet him when he returned later that same day. It was just as she rounded the corner of his block and was basking in thoughts of her beloved that she saw a young couple swing out from under the portico of his building.

It was Charles — and a stunningly beautiful blonde. Jane watched in shock as Charles leaned close to the woman, whispered something that made her trill with laughter, then threw his arm around her and led her to his car parked at the kerb. And when they were both settled inside, the man of her dreams reached over, drew his adoring companion into his arms and kissed her — lingeringly. Then they roared off into the late-morning sun.

Jane had registered the whole scene as if in a nightmare. She turned and began to run. Where, she wasn't sure, for where do you run when your whole world has just collapsed?

Despite Charles's attempts to call her over the next few days, Jane refused to see or talk to him. Eventually he gave up, and Jane hadn't seen him since.

She vowed never to let herself be fooled by a man again. Of course this resolve meant not letting any man get too close. The scar on her heart became like a seal, which Edna's lectures served only to harden. She did allow some men into her life, men like Fred. But apart from brief kisses, occasional hand holding, their relationship was platonic. Fred no doubt hoped things would eventually move on to another, more intimate plane, and who knew? Maybe, with time, it would.

At last it was closing time. Jane crossed to the front door and locked it, then rang up the purchases of the last two remaining customers and sent them on their way with a smile and pleasant good-bye, which she managed to summon convincingly.

She stopped on the way home to pick up some groceries, a task she always found cheering. A stir-fry of vegetables and some leftover chicken from the previous night's dinner would make a good meal, one Deirdre would enjoy, too, she thought with satisfaction. Thanks to her aunt's cooking, the girl was developing a taste for foods that were exotic as well as nourishing, which according to Sharon had been as likely as vacation on Neptune.

At nine o'clock Jane was standing in

her kitchen watching the rice turn to glue. Deirdre should have been home an hour ago. Jane couldn't believe this was happening again. Granted, nine o'clock was a far cry from midnight, but still, it had only been four days since that last episode. Surely to heaven there wasn't going to be a repeat of Monday night!

No, there definitely would not, Jane decided angrily, whipping off her apron. Seymour yowled in protest as she nearly tripped over his languorous form stretched out in the doorway between the kitchen and sitting-room. "Sorry, big boy, but get out of my way. I've got things to do."

★ ★ ★

"Yes, may I help you?"

The heavy oak door had swung open to reveal Joss, Dominic Slater's silver-haired assistant. Jane wondered if the woman's face was ever anything other than impatient and irritable. She decided she didn't care.

"Yes, you can. By letting me in!" And with that, Jane pushed past a spluttering Joss and crossed the hallway to the door she knew opened into the studio.

"You can't go in there!" shouted Joss.

Jane ignored her and entered to see Dom crouched on the floor with a hand-held camera, following the wild contortions of his subject. She was tall and blonde, lithe and beautiful. And she wasn't Deirdre.

At Jane's entrance, all action stopped. Heads swivelled in her direction. Jane swallowed, momentarily struck dumb. Dom, still crouched, was the first to speak. He glared at her and snarled, "What the — " then directed this gaze back to his model, his tone soothing. "Okay, Lila, take a break."

He stood, then strode furiously over to plant himself in front of Jane. "And to what, may I ask, do I owe the pleasure of your visit this time,

Ms Cuthbert? Is Lila another one of your innocent nieces? Did you expect to witness a ritual deflowering? Is your mouth hanging open in disappointment, or are you just hoping to catch flies?"

Jane snapped her mouth shut and took a deep, calming breath through her nostrils. "It's Cathcart. And I apologize — " Jane nearly choked on the word " — for having to interrupt you at work, but Deirdre seems to have gone missing, and — "

"I'm not the last person to have seen her alive?" He gave a mirthless laugh.

"It's no joke!" Jane returned angrily. "Deirdre was going to call me if you were keeping her late, and she hasn't called, and it is late, so I assumed she — "

" — was here at my studio, or perhaps upstairs in my boudoir being ravished — "

"Stop it!" Jane shrieked, her tenuous hold on her control lost. "How dare you make fun of me!"

And then she burst into tears.

Instantly Dom was at her side, thrusting a spotless linen handkerchief in the direction of her nose. "Okay, okay, er, Jane, isn't it?"

At her weak nod, Dom waved an arm at the people on the set. "Folks, I think we've got what we want, so let's pack up. Lila, you were fantastic, and I'll call you if I think we need to do any more. Go home and get some sleep for that beautiful face of yours. You, too, Joss. Thanks for your help, as usual."

Jane's hysteria had subsided enough by now to take in some of this. She couldn't help but note how the lion had turned into a lamb. But it was not to last.

He switched his attention sharply back to Jane. "So," he snarled, "I see you've recovered somewhat. Maybe now you can behave like a rational human being. Or is it too presumptuous of me to imagine that you're capable of such a feat?"

Jane could see a muscle twitch in

his hardened jaw, a vein throb in his forehead. She actually trembled as she mumbled, "I'm quite capable."

"Fine. Now as one human being to another, I'd like to know exactly what brings you here. Why you seem to think I'm responsible for Dee's welfare. I haven't seen her since she left my studio at six o'clock."

Jane gasped. "Six o'clock? But it's almost ten now. She promised to call if she was going to be late. Maybe something terrible's happened to her. Maybe — "

"Stop!" Dominic roared. "I get enough hysterics from some of my models. I don't need them from you."

"I apologize for getting upset on your precious premises," Jane snapped. "Clearly I've come to the wrong place for help — not that I should expect any from the likes of you!"

"The likes . . . look, I know it's fun to trade insults, but perhaps now isn't the time."

Jane felt immediately contrite. "No, it isn't. Forgive me. I . . . I'm not quite myself . . . "

"It's okay . . . Jane, I'm sure Dee is fine. I think it's entirely possible she's gone somewhere with Gineen."

"Gineen?"

"Gineen Kendrick, another model who was on the shoot today with Dee. She's a bit older than Dee, and more, uh, worldly. Kind of knows her way around town. Maybe she's taken Dee to one of her favourite haunts. They did seem to hit it off . . . "

"Where? Where might they go? Tell me. I'll go there and — "

"Jane, hold it. I'll do better than tell you. I'll go there with you."

Jane glanced at him in surprise. "Mr Slater — "

"Dom."

She made a sound of exasperation. "Dom. That won't be necessary. Deirdre isn't your responsibility, she's mine."

"On the contrary, Jane. I've just had second thoughts about Dee's welfare, since I, and her agent, and the clients, have a vested interest in her. She's a valuable property."

"She's a damn sight more than a valuable property! She's also a sweet and impressionable young girl, with family who love and worry about her, and if anything were to happen — "

"Spare me. I get the picture. Come on, let's get out of here. You need my help, because going into some of these joints Gineen thinks are cool isn't a job for a little librarian from small-town America."

"I am not a librarian! I run my own business, a bookshop, and I do know my way around town!"

"Shhh. I'm teasing. I'm beginning to see you're not quite what you appear."

As Jane debated whether to feel complimented or insulted by that last cryptic remark, Dom reached out a hand, and with his forefinger, drew a line down her flushed cheek. She leapt back as if his finger were made of molten lead. Dom shook his head in apparent puzzlement, then moved away.

"First," he announced, "I'll call Gineen's place. I'll see if she's there. See if they're both there. I know Gineen well, and I know she hates going out alone." Then he left Jane standing in the hallway, somewhat dazed — and then mindful of his words.

He knew Gineen well, he'd said. Did that mean he'd dated her? Seemed likely, and didn't that confirm her suspicions about the relationship between a photographer and his model — that it was natural, almost inevitable, to carry on the intimacy of a photo shoot outside the studio?

"Got her answering machine," Dom said, striding back into the hallway. "A good sign." Before Jane could question that judgement, he placed his hand briefly on her shoulder and gave it a squeeze, and this time Jane did not leap away. There was something almost reassuring about the touch.

"Let's get going," he said, grasping

her elbow and leading her to the door. "First stop," he announced, "Lord Byron's."

Jane didn't know whether to feel relieved or worried at not finding Deirdre at the trendy uptown club. Relieved because her niece was too young for the Lord Byron crowd, not to mention too young to drink, and worried because if she was with this Gineen, and Gineen liked these places, then where were they?

Dom had hailed another cab, and despite her anxiety about Deirdre, Jane found herself annoyed at the ease with which he'd done so. She gave herself a mental shake. The sooner they found Deirdre the better, and if Dominic Slater seemed to be one of those for whom the seas parted, then she ought to be grateful. Besides, after tonight, she'd probably never see him again.

"Louis Quatorze," Dom ordered the cabbie. Jane thought she detected an odd note in his voice and she felt a little whizz of fear. What kind of place

38

was Louis Quatorze?

When she asked Dom, his reply was an enigmatic, "You'll see. All will be revealed. It's not far, and I heard Gineen mention the place the other day. Good chance they'll be there." He patted Jane's hand. Annoyed, she snatched it away.

Did he have to be so ... so patronizing? So sure of himself? And, said a voice inside her, so damned attractive? For Jane was finding the close confines of the cabs they'd shared more than a little disconcerting. His nearness was doing strange things to her. Things she hadn't felt since Charles. Things she never wanted to feel again.

She shifted her body away from him. Just enough to keep her thigh from brushing his every time the cab turned a corner, but not enough so he'd notice ...

But of course he did.

"Jane," he said dryly, "do you really find me so repulsive? Unfortunately cabs are places that rather force a certain intimacy between occupants."

Was it her imagination, or did he actually pause slightly before and after the word 'intimacy', dragging the sibilant syllables out, making the word sound like a caress? As she struggled to phrase an appropriate comeback, he said, "Look, relax, for God's sake. I'm not in the habit of making passes at women who obviously dislike my company. Besides, you're — " a pause " — hardly my type."

Jane should have felt relieved, but instead she felt as if she'd been slapped in the face. No, she wasn't a tall lissom beauty, nothing at all like the models he preferred. Maybe she wasn't an instant head-turner like Sharon or Deirdre, but she wasn't a complete washout in the looks department. Charles had been fond of calling her 'small but sultry', Edna thought she resembled a romantic heroine, and Fred . . . well, Fred's admiration of her was written plainly all over his face.

She recalled suddenly something else Deirdre had told her about Dominic. Six or seven years earlier, he'd had a brief and stormy — if the tabloids were to be believed — marriage to Katya Simms, an internationally famous model. Jane had heard of Katya; it was impossible not to, for the press loved her. Her name and photo were splashed frequently in national newspapers and magazines, and she'd been linked with a number of equally glamorous, usually rich, movie stars, oil barons, and the like. Jane couldn't imagine what had caused the split between her and Dominic, but obviously it was the beautiful Katyas of this world he was attracted to, not the plain Janes.

But what really irked her about his comment, however, was none of the above. At the root of the problem was the fact that while he was supremely indifferent to her, she was anything but indifferent to him . . .

3

JANE was aghast. "Deirdre wouldn't go to a place like this! I can't go in there!"

She and Dominic were standing in front of Louis Quatorze. Above the heads of the tittering young women in the line-up was a marquee with the bold slogan: EXOTIC MALE DANCERS.

"Perhaps not on her own, Ms Cathcart, but she might with the daring Ms Kendrick." The expression on his face was amusement — at her expense, Jane fumed. But she'd meant what she'd said. Couldn't he go in there by himself and look around? Did he really need her? She voiced her questions aloud.

"There are few places in the world for which I have any qualm about entering by myself," he replied. "This, however, is one of them. Men, at least men of my persuasion, do not go to see male strippers. I need a woman with me to, er, validate my masculinity."

Jane gave him an assessing look and thought, if ever there was a man whose masculinity could never be in doubt, it was Dominic Slater. Nevertheless she took his point, and gained a certain satisfaction in the knowledge that his seemingly unperturbable self could be unhinged, however slightly, by anything. The idea made her smile. "All right, let's do it."

"Atta girl. And who knows? Maybe you'll learn something."

Jane felt like slapping his handsome, grinning face.

After a word with the doorman, Dom and Jane were allowed entry; Jane cringed at the wrathful glances they received from the women waiting in line, but Dominic grasped her arm and propelled her before him into the club.

The interior was as foreign to Jane as the lunar landscape. It was jammed with squealing women of all ages. The music had a pounding primitive beat, and through the haze of smoke and maze of tables, an almost nude muscular young man could be seen thrusting his pelvis forward and back in a manner that was more than suggestive; to Jane it was obscene.

Dominic tapped her on the shoulder. Bending so that his mouth was to her ear, he said, "Look. There she is," and pointed to an area on the other side of the stage. Jane followed the direction of his finger and spotted Deirdre. She was sharing a tiny table with a pair of young women, both dark-haired, both possessing model-like beauty, and both in perhaps their late teens or early twenties. Deirdre, unlike her more sophisticated companions, had her widened eyes glued on the stripper, her lovely mouth hanging open in what appeared to be delighted shock.

Jane started to head in Deirdre's direction, but Dominic held her back and said almost kindly, as if sensing her very real abhorrence of the place, "Wait here, or better yet just outside. I'll get Dee."

"She's my . . . " Jane began, but the leering gestures of the stripper made her think better of it. "Okay," she said, and as Dom continued to make his way between the tables of enthralled females, she turned toward the entrance.

The few minutes she waited on the sidewalk felt like for ever. When at last the pair emerged, Jane found that her worry about Deirdre had metamorphosed into sheer anger; she wanted to strangle her. Dom had moved to the kerb, hailed a cab, and was now gesturing for Jane and Deirdre to get in. But he himself remained on the sidewalk road and, before closing the door behind them, said, "I don't think I'm needed now. See you next week, Dee."

Despite her agitation, Jane remembered her manners. She rolled down her window. "Dom, wait a minute. I want to thank — "

"Forget it," he said curtly. Then he seemed to undergo a change of mood. He gave Jane one of his award-winning smiles and reached through the window to touch her arm. "I don't get the chance very often to play Sir Galahad. It was a pleasure. Sort of." His eyes, glimmering with wry humour, caught and held hers for the briefest of moments before the cab pulled away.

"Oh, Jane, I'm sorry — " began Deirdre, the moment Jane was settled in her seat.

"We'll talk about this when we get home, Deirdre. If I listen to you now I can't be held accountable for my actions." The implication was that Jane was so angry she might attempt to throw Deirdre from the moving cab, but in truth, her inner turmoil at that moment had little to do with her errant niece. What she really needed was a few minutes to compose herself, to collect and consider the feelings *Dominic* had stirred up in her.

Deirdre heaved a great sigh and fell back against the vinyl. She did, however, glance nervously from time to time at Jane. Oh, let her worry for a bit, thought Jane peevishly. I've done my share.

After they'd climbed the two flights of stairs, entered the apartment and Jane had latched all three locks, she turned to her niece. "Okay, miss. Start explaining." While her voice sounded calm, it masked an astonishing tumult of emotions, a mix of anger and hurt, puzzlement and relief.

To her amazement, Deirdre's response was to burst into tears. Jane frantically fished in her bag for some tissues. "Here," she said, poking a clutch of them at Deirdre. Then she put a comforting arm around her and led her to the sofa. "I don't know why you're crying, sweetie. You're too old for a spanking, and I can hardly cut off your allowance."

Jane's feeble attempt at humour was lost on Deirdre, whose sobbing only increased. Jane recalled old movies where a person in hysterics could be cured with a slap. Tempted, but thinking better of if, she tried another tack. "Deirdre!" she said in a voice that would have done credit to a platoon sergeant.

Startled, Deirdre looked up and her sobs tapered to sniffles. She put a tissue to her nose and gave a thorough blow, and then turned tear-reddened eyes to her aunt. "Oh, Jane, I'm sorry. I didn't drink anything alcoholic, honest, and I meant to call, I really did, but I lost track of the time and — "

"Do not give me that line again. We went through this the other night, and you promised! Or don't your promises mean anything to you? I thought you were better than that."

Her niece hung her head and muttered something unintelligible.

"What, Deirdre?" Jane asked. "What did you say?"

"I said," the girl repeated miserably, "that I couldn't, just couldn't, call you

48

when I was with Gineen and Debbie. They're so smart and grown-up and . . . and . . . I felt like one of them. I *was* one of them! So how could I excuse myself to call home, when that kind of stuff's only for kids?"

"Sure, Deirdre, fine, but the ironic thing is that if you were really grown-up you'd keep your promises and not be so concerned about what others think of you. You owed me a call at the very least, and, well, I'm just really disappointed in you."

At the truly stricken look on her niece's face, Jane relented. "Aw, come on, Deirdre. It's not the end of the world." She paused, then asked, "And why were you crying so hard? I mean, I'm not *that* much of an ogre, am I? Is there something I've missed?" Please, dear Lord, let there not be, she thought. I've had enough for one night.

"Well," Deirdre began hesitantly, "have you ever been humiliated in front of . . . by . . . someone you love?"

Jane was taken aback. "What are you talking about, Deirdre? Who humiliated you?"

"Well, he didn't mean to humiliate me, Jane. And it wasn't really awful, except I was pretty embarrassed, but when he walked up and . . . and then in front of Gineen and Debbie . . . "

Something lurched inside Jane. "Wait a minute. Are you saying you *love* Dominic Slater?"

"Oh, yes, Jane, I really do!" she breathed. "And I'm not being silly. I know he feels something for me, too, so when he came up to the table and sort of had to take me away like a naughty little girl, saying my aunt was waiting, and . . . oh! I was so embarrassed!"

"Deirdre, honey, what you feel for Dominic isn't love. It's just a crush."

"No, it's not! It's the real thing. And I'm sure he feels the same way — or close to it! I can tell by the way he treats me. And he even cared enough to come out looking for me tonight."

The girl paused and her eyes narrowed.

"In fact, why did *you* have to be there? If you hadn't been, then maybe he would've taken me home, and maybe he would've kissed me, and — "

"Deirdre! Are you telling me he's kissed you before?"

"Well, sort of."

"Sort of? What does *that* mean, sort of?"

"Well, he gives me a kiss sometimes after a good session."

"What! He does?"

"Yes . . . " She coloured. "Well, it's just a quickie, you know, sort of a thank-you — but I know he'd like to *really* kiss me . . . "

"Oh, Deirdre, no, honey, no. He likes you of course. But you're much too young for him. Can't you see that?"

Yet even as she spoke Jane wasn't at all sure that Dominic had any scruples about the age of the women he dated. He'd implied that he'd dated Gineen, and while Gineen was a little older than Deirdre, she was still many years his junior. Jane wondered about his kissing models on the set. Was that something he made a habit of? Did it mean anything?

Deirdre twisted angrily away from her aunt's touch. "No! He's not that much older — maybe thirty-five. There're lots of marriages between people with twenty years' difference in their ages. Lots! I'll be sixteen soon, and I'm his type, too!"

You're hardly my type . . . Jane closed her eyes as his words floated unpleasantly back to her.

Deirdre went on, "I've seen pictures of Katya, his ex-wife, and we really look alike. I've heard he still carries a . . . a . . . "

"Torch?"

"Yeah, torch for her, and I know I can be the one to make him forget all about her." Deirdre's face and voice took on an almost religious fervour as she added, "I know I'm right for him. I just know it."

"Oh, Deirdre," Jane said again, but

her niece wasn't quite finished. She had one more card to play.

"He wouldn't go looking for just any model, and I don't believe he did just because of *you*. He did it for me, and . . . it shows he loves me!"

A short time later, as she got ready for bed, Jane was certain her sleep, which was light at the best of times, would be non-existent tonight. Deirdre's feelings for Dominic were classic infatuation, Jane knew — she'd suffered from the same syndrome herself when she was a teenager, but at least her idols had been so far out of reach her parents hadn't had a thing to worry about. But in Deirdre's case . . .

Dom did have a reputation for dating models; he'd even married one. How could she be sure he was hands-off Deirdre? Lord knew the girl looked much older than she was. It was easy for anyone to forget she was just a kid. And Deirdre so desperately wanted to be taken for an adult that she tried, and often succeeded in, behaving like one.

Yet, despite the fact that Dom seemed able to cast a spell on every female he encountered, something about him told Jane he *was* hands-off someone as young as her niece. Now if only Deirdre would get over her crush. Were crushes curable? Was adolescence? Yes, Jane thought, it just took time. Besides, her niece would be going home when summer was over, and that would be the end of this nonsense. Yet Jane felt a tiny pinprick of worry in that direction, too. After all, Deirdre would be sixteen in another couple of months and therefore legally allowed to leave school and leave home. Surely, Jane thought, the girl wasn't foolish enough to do that.

Jane resolved to discuss the troubling situation with Fred. They were getting together for dinner and an off-Broadway play tomorrow night, and Fred was possessed of a good deal of common sense. His feet were planted squarely on the ground, and he was good at lending an ear and giving advice.

Suddenly an image of Dominic Slater flashed through her mind. To Jane's surprise he, too, had shown himself capable of common sense; it was thanks to him they'd found Deirdre. But traits like common sense and feet planted squarely on the ground were hardly the first things that jumped to mind when Jane thought of the photographer. No, what did run riot in her head were his assessing cool blue eyes, his sensual mouth, his powerful body, his . . . *presence*. A sum total that shook her peace of mind, and made her feel things she thought she'd put behind her for ever.

4

THE next morning, Saturday, as Jane prepared her usual breakfast of wheatgerm-sprinkled granola, the Deirdre who sat up and stretched was sweetly apologetic.

"Jane, I really am sorry about last night." Then her enormous blue eyes blinked rapidly, and her young mouth quivered. "You're not gonna tell Mom, are you? You know how she gets . . . "

Indeed Jane did. There was every chance that, if Sharon knew of her daughter's escapade, she'd demand that Deirdre get on the first plane back to Dubuque.

Still, she nodded and said, "It's okay, Deirdre. I won't, but this behaviour twice in one week . . . It's too much. Not again. If it does, I'm sending you home. I don't want to have to do that, but I will."

Deirdre could see that her aunt had been pushed as far as she'd go. The girl scrambled off the pulled-out couch, then crossed to Jane. "Thanks for giving me one more chance." Deirdre threw her arms around her aunt and hugged her. "You're the best, Jane. I won't let you down. Promise."

"Okay." Jane gave her niece a hug in return.

"So, are you seeing Fred tonight? What are you gonna be doing?" Deirdre asked some minutes later when they were sitting over second cups of fresh-ground coffee.

Bemused by her niece's interest, Jane said, "Yes, he's meeting me here after I get back from the shop — around 6.30."

"He's so sweet, Jane," Deirdre said. "I'm glad you've got a guy like that."

"Me, too," murmured Jane. What had brought this on? she wondered. Her niece had never made a comment about Fred one way or the other before, in fact if anything had seemed totally unimpressed with Jane's choice of male companion.

"He's super, Jane!" Deirdre went on. "Hey, what do you say I meet you during your lunch break and we go shopping? You need a new outfit, something neat, not like . . . "

The dull stuff she usually wore, Jane knew Deirdre wanted to say. She sighed. "I don't have much time at lunch, you know . . . "

"Come on, Jane. Nancy can take care of the Book Nook for an hour, can't she? I saw this fantastic shop on Third the other day with these really neat clothes."

Nancy Barstow, Jane knew, was more than capable of handling the bookstore on her own for a while — even on a busy Saturday. A recent English graduate from Columbia University, Nancy was a lot like Jane in many ways. A pretty dark-haired girl, she loved books, had a friendly yet business-like attitude with customers, a generally cautious approach to life, and apparently spent much of her leisure time just keeping up with the latest books. Jane had never heard her talk about men, and so she assumed Nancy didn't even have a current relationship. Cheerful and unassuming, she was the perfect employee. Jane trusted her completely.

Still, Jane wasn't big on shopping for clothes, and she wasn't sure that Deirdre's idea of 'neat' coincided with her own. Nevertheless, she said at last, "Okay, meet me at the Book Nook at noon."

"All right!"

Jane went off to work shaking her head in amazement at the enviable resilience of the young.

★ ★ ★

"You look, uh . . . unusual, Jane." Fred's eyes blinked rapidly as he spoke. "New outfit? And I've never seen you wear your hair that way before . . . "

As if her appearance were too much

for him, Fred bent awkwardly at the knee to stroke Seymour. The cat responded instantly with a graceless little squawk and a hasty escape to Jane's bedroom, and Jane almost felt like applauding her pet's rudeness. She wasn't the sort of woman who craved male admiration, but for once she'd spent time and money in an effort to look good, and a compliment would have been nice. This afternoon's purchase — a vivid red-and-black belted tunic and contour-hugging black Capris pants — was not the sort of thing she usually wore, true, but Jane felt right in the outfit. It was, as the spike-haired salesgirl had pointed out, *her*.

And Deirdre, bless her, had spent half an hour styling her hair. She'd brushed it back from Jane's forehead and temples, then secured it magically in place with combs, an art Jane had previously attempted, but never mastered.

"Thanks, Fred," Jane replied dryly.

Fred, tall, slim and sandy-haired, was conservative in manner and appearance; in fact it was partly his conservation that she valued him for, so why rebuke him for it now? If he found her appearance tonight a little excessive for his tastes, well, they were in agreement on most other things. Things that counted.

Anyway, her outfit was appropriate for the evening's activities — dinner at a bistro, followed by an *avant garde*, off-Broadway play, which Fred had heard was particularly good. Despite his conservative attitude about many things, he had an appreciation for original and unusual art — in films and plays, paintings and music — which usually mirrored Jane's.

"Let's get going, Fred. The play starts at 8.30 and if we're going to have time to eat . . . "

"Have a great time, you guys," called Deirdre through a mouthful of bran muffin. She sauntered into the living-room from the kitchen. "I'll be asleep by the time you're home, so don't worry about waking me — I sleep like a log," she said, and then, not looking at her aunt but at Fred, added, "Of course, that is, *if* you guys come back here . . . "

Oh great, thought Jane. It was one thing for her niece to perform the nudge-nudge-wink-wink routine for her, as she'd done a couple of times while they were shopping and while she was fixing Jane's hair, but, please, not for Fred.

★ ★ ★

"Yes, of course, Jane, I'd be worried, too. Deirdre's way too young for a guy like that, in fact no woman would be safe with him."

Fred's look implied that she, too, was in danger. Jane closed her eyes briefly and finished her *café au lait*. During dinner, she'd told Fred about her niece and the goings-on of the night before, and was disappointed to realize she didn't feel at all unburdened. What was it about her two encounters with the black-haired, blue-eyed photographer that wouldn't give her any peace of mind? Did she really have to fear for Deirdre?

No, that wasn't it, not exactly. Dom wasn't about to pounce on her niece — especially now that he knew the girl's age and the fact she had a protective aunt. But Deirdre's feelings for Dom were the problem. Fred's assurance that her crush would pass hadn't helped. Fred, after all, hadn't met the man.

The little theatre was full, and Jane found the two-act play not especially to her liking. It was one of those plays about *life*, and seemed to be trying to make a statement that was as profound as it was incomprehensible. She was glad when the first act was over and she and Fred made their way out into the crowded lobby for a drink. Her eyes scanned the theatre-goers, and she was gratified at least to see that her figure-hugging, red-and-black clothing fitted right in.

Oh, no! Please, let my eyes be deceiving me. There in a far corner of the lobby was the last person she wanted to see. Dominic Slater, and clinging to him like porous plaster, a striking young woman whose height, perfect bones, stylish hairdo and flawless complexion showed her to be a model.

And just as Jane spotted him, he caught her eye. She looked away quickly, hoping against hope he hadn't recognized her, or if he had, would choose to ignore her. But it was not to be. Damn. And the intermission had only just begun. Double damn.

He arrived at her side, his date in tow, at the same time as Fred returned with a couple of fruit drinks. "So, how do you like the play so far?" were Dom's first words.

They were addressed to Jane, but Fred, acting in a manner that was quite unlike him, answered before Jane had a chance to open her mouth. "An astonishing piece of work," he said. "The playwright has a real sense of the iconoclastic nature of — "

"I think it's a pretentious piece of iconoclastic junk," Dominic interjected.

Jane stifled a groan, while Dom's date merely looked about the room, her expression one of mild boredom. Jane wished she could do the same, for the tension between the two men was almost palpable. Why had Dom felt it necessary to be so disagreeable? And to Fred, who had done nothing to deserve such treatment beyond, perhaps, speaking out of turn. Why, come to that, had Dominic made his way over to her at all?

She thought it wise to run some interference. "Now, come on. It isn't exactly junk. Maybe it is rather pretentious — " she turned apologetically to Fred " — but I think the playwright makes some sort of point about an artist's battle between intellect and feeling. I'm just not sure what it is!" Jane gave a little peal of laughter, hoping to relieve the tension.

She wasn't a raging success. Fred merely looked at her in stony silence, and Dominic regarded her with an unfathomable expression. It might have been respect; it might just as easily have been disdain.

Suddenly Dominic smiled. "Jane," he said, ignoring Fred, "you look . . . terrific." His gaze ran up and down her in a way Jane would have found insulting had it come from any other man. She decided the reason she didn't take offence was that Dom had a professional eye for women, and so a scrutiny and a compliment from him were almost flattering, especially after Fred's less than effective reaction to her appearance earlier.

"Thank you," she said, with an answering smile, feeling more than seeing the murderous look on Fred's face. Maybe his anger was justified, though.

"Fred, this is Dominic Slater,

Deirdre's photog — "

"So I've gathered," Fred put in coolly, extending his hand. "And I'm Fred Anderson. Jane's told me a lot about you, and as soon as I saw your lovely companion — " Fred slid a glance her way " — I could see she must be a model, and so . . . "

He said the words in a way that implied a certain disapproval, which made Jane wish she'd stayed home that evening and watched a movie on TV with Deirdre. Vaguely she wondered if Dom was even going to introduce the young woman by his side. She seemed quite uninterested in Jane and Fred, her gaze still shifting about the room — though, Jane noticed, her slender, perfectly manicured fingers rested possessively on Dominic's arm.

Jane was surprised at the peculiar little jolt of dismay she felt when Dom looped an arm familiarly over his date's shoulder, smiled warmly at her and introduced her as "Karen — one of my favourite models. I see, Mr Anderson, that you have an eye for beauty."

Dominic's glance flicked to Jane for the briefest of moments, then away. She had an idea, quickly abandoned, that his comment didn't refer only to Karen. Fred suddenly seemed to recognize an opportunity for gallantry. Echoing Dominic, he reached for Jane and pulled her close to his side. "Indeed I do, Mr Slater." He smiled down at Jane. "Indeed I do."

Jane thought she was going to throw up.

★ ★ ★

The following Wednesday was not a particularly hectic day at the Book Nook, but Jane found she was getting a headache. When Fred dropped by at noon to see if she wanted to go out for a bite at the local deli, she turned him down. "I'd be terrible company — I've got a splitting headache. Feels like the

68

Battle of Little Big Horn was fought there."

Fred smiled thinly, but still seemed determined to convince her. "Come on, Jane. A couple of aspirin and a cup of tea will set you right."

Jane massaged the bridge of her nose. She liked Fred, but disliked it when he got insistent, which, thank heaven, he didn't do often. Although, she recalled, just last Saturday night after the play, he had. He'd asked her to come up to his apartment for "a nightcap — I've got some of your favourite liqueur, or tea, if you'd rather, a new flavour you'll love." She'd had to spend a good ten minutes during the cab ride explaining her refusal, and then apologizing for it, before Fred finally let her off the hook.

Suddenly an idea occurred to her. "Why don't you go out with Nancy for lunch?" She turned toward her assistant, who was standing on a stool placing books on one of the higher shelves. "What do you say, Nance?

69

Want to keep Fred here company? You two can talk about the latest Frank Lowe book Fred has just contracted. It's coming out next spring and I hear it's great . . . "

"Sure, no problem. Glad to," Nancy said. Thank heaven Nancy was so agreeable, thought Jane.

She was kept pretty busy during the lunch-hour, and her headache retreated. She knew its cause — tension. For in the past few days Deirdre had resumed her prattle about Dominic Slater. Jane's hope that her niece would come to her senses and see that what she felt for the photographer was just a temporary infatuation had not come to pass. If anything her niece seemed more convinced than ever that love was there, and if Dominic had yet to fully realize it, well, he would. It was a topic Jane was thoroughly weary of.

Only the night before, Jane decided it was in Deirdre's best interests to tell her about seeing Dominic on Saturday night with a date. She'd refrained earlier, reluctant to engage with her niece in any sort of conversation about Dominic's love life. Deirdre, to her surprise, had taken the news quite nonchalantly.

"Oh, I know he *dates* lots of women, Jane. But he doesn't *care* about them. And I've heard about Karen — she just likes to be seen with him. It's good for her career, to be seen dating a famous photographer, going to the right places . . . She hasn't got any interest in him personally. He hasn't got any interest in her, either."

But even as Deirdre spouted her sophisticated phrases, Jane saw a look of pain flash across her young features. She decided not to mention the way Karen had clung to Dominic, the way he had put his arm around her and pulled her close. The last thing she wanted was to see her niece hurt. But there just didn't seem to be a simple, kind way to help her avoid it. Jane just prayed things would run their course.

When Jane arrived home that evening,

she was met by a blast of rock music, accompanied by Deirdre's high, off-key, voice coming from the kitchen, from where also came an enticing spicy smell of food cooking. She hollered a greeting as she bent to pick up Seymour.

"Is that you, Jane?"

"Of course. Who else? Ghengis Khan?"

"When is what?" Deirdre shouted.

"Nothing." Jane sighed, extracting Seymour's claws from her blouse and returning him to the floor. She marched over to the stereo set to turn down the volume, ignoring Deirdre's wail of protest.

Then she smiled as her nostrils again picked up the aroma wafting from the kitchen. "What are you up to in there?" she said. "Smells great."

"Come in here. I've got to keep stirring this stuff or it'll burn."

When Jane wandered into the kitchen, she was struck anew by her niece's loveliness. Even though Deirdre was dressed in jeans and a baggy shirt, her face bare of make-up, she still exuded a sensuality that was as natural to her as eating or sleeping. It was almost impossible to think of her as a child.

Deirdre switched off the stove element and turned a flushed and glowing face to her aunt. "There, it's done. You're gonna love this meal. It's Mexican. Got the stuff over at that specialty-food shop around the corner, and I've been following the recipes in one of your cookbooks."

"Looks yummy, Deirdre. And what, may I ask, has stirred you to such ambitious heights of culinary delights, hmm?"

Deirdre giggled and waved the spoon she was still holding. "Oh, Jane, wait'll I tell you. You're just gonna die!"

"Okay, sweetie, lay it on me. You've just won the lottery? Michael Jackson called to beg for your hand in marriage?"

Deirdre giggled again. "Oh, yuck, no way! No, something even better! My agent wants me to go on a shoot in Mexico! The Yutacan!"

"That's Yucatan, I believe."

"Yeah, right. Whatever." She waved a dismissing hand. "And guess what?" Deirdre's eyes shone. "The photographer is going to be Dom!"

Jane's stomach lurched. It was one thing to deal with Deirdre's passion for the photographer here in New York where she could keep an eye on her. But Mexico? "Great, Deirdre, but have you told your mom? I'm not sure she'll approve . . ."

"Oh, Jane, I knew you'd say that. You're just like Mom." In her present position as Deirdre's guardian, Jane took that as a compliment. "Anyway," Deirdre went on, "I thought maybe you could call her for me and tell her I can look after myself. Besides it's only one week and I won't be on my own. Dom will be there, and Joss, and someone from the fashion designers', and . . ."

Jane didn't bother to mention that

the fact Dom would be there was anything but reassuring. Then Deirdre added, "You wouldn't believe what they're paying for this job. Enough for a year at college that should convince Mom and Dad."

Yes, thought Jane, it probably should. Sharon and Bill wanted their kids to attend college, but they weren't exactly flush with money.

"Will you call them now, Jane? Please? My agent needs to know right away if I can go, and — "

"Yes, okay, Deirdre. But we're on different time zones, don't forget, and they're probably not home from work yet."

Deirdre flung her arms around her aunt. "Jane, you're the best! I know you'll convince Mom."

As she gently extracted herself from her exuberant niece's hold, Jane considered her dilemma. On the one hand she thought the opportunity was, financially, too good for Deirdre to miss. On the other, it was like a green light to loss of innocence — and heartbreak.

A couple of hours later, Jane sat on her bed, having just hung up the phone after a conversation with Sharon. Deirdre burst into the room almost before Jane had replaced the receiver in its cradle.

"How'd it go, Jane? What'd she say? Is it okay?"

"Hold on there a second, Deirdre. Your mother says yes, but — "

"Yippee!" Deirdre shrieked, jumping up and down like a 6-year-old. "I knew she'd listen to you." Then, apparently remembering she was supposed to be an adult, and that meant displaying a little decorum, she stopped. "But?"

"She insists I go to Mexico with you."

"What? What? No way. I don't need a chaperone! I'm old enough to take care of myself!"

"Be that as it may, Deirdre, my going is the only way your mother will agree to let you go. And I'm not sure I *can*. I have to give this a little thought. I told your mother I'd call her tomorrow night, and I will. Can your agent wait a couple of days to get your answer?"

Deirdre groaned. "Oh, I can't believe this! How can I say to my agent that I have to get *Mommy's* permission? This is so embarrassing. I — "

"Put on the brakes, Deirdre. And look on the bright side. Your mother's initial response to your flying off to Mexico was no. When I told her about the fee you'd receive for the job, she suddenly came up with a solution. You go, I go."

"So will you, Jane? Will you?"

Could she really have a vacation if she had to chaperone Deirdre? Sharon had pooh-poohed that reservation. Yes, it *would* be a vacation. Deirdre would be busy working most of the time, and after all she wasn't a baby. And wasn't midsummer a slow time for book sales and so relatively safe to leave the shop for a spell? Hadn't Jane told her she had a great assistant?

Jane had responded with a reluctant yes to all of Sharon's questions, and finally agreed to think seriously about the idea. Maybe she could swing the vacation time, maybe Nancy could handle the shop. Maybe she could get someone, Fred or a neighbour perhaps, to come by every day and feed Seymour. But how could she really enjoy herself when she found Dominic's presence so unsettling, Deirdre's crush so disturbing?

"I told you I have to think about it."

Deirdre pouted. "Well, the job's less than two weeks away — but I guess my agent can wait a couple of days."

Her expression became pleading. "Oh, Aunt Jane, you know I'll behave from now on. I remember my promise. I won't give you anything to worry about if you go to Mexico. You'll get a vacation, and you'll get to see all those, uh, Aztec ruins — "

"Mayan," Jane corrected.

" — and beaches, and — " Deirdre's

eyes gleamed at her own brilliant inspiration " — clean air!"

Clean air, thought Jane, yes, that was certainly a plus, but in this case, it was the least of the deciding factors. "I'll make up my mind tomorrow, Deirdre. Don't push me, okay?"

Tossing her aunt a glare of frustration, Deirdre flung her head in a motion that swirled her hair in a wild glorious arc, and stomped from the room.

Jane turned to Seymour, stretched out languorously on the bedspread, and said, "What, I ask you, did I do to deserve all this? Huh? Tell me."

Seymour blinked open one yellow eye, then gave a soft groan and fell instantly back to sleep.

5

JANE was standing precariously on the stool, trying to place a book on one of the upper shelves. The spot was maddeningly just out of reach.

"Need a hand?"

Jane twisted her head to see who had spoken and nearly fell off the stool.

"Steady there," said Dominic. "I've heard industrial accidents are one of the leading causes of deaths for small women in this country."

"Oh, please!" said Jane exasperatedly. Her heart began to beat alarmingly. "If you hadn't snuck up on me like that, I'd be fine!"

"You don't look fine." He took in her wilder-than-usual hair, her flushed face, her untucked blouse. "You look as if you're in training for a high-wire act."

He reached up then, grasped a

spluttering Jane about the waist and pulled her to the floor. "There. Now give me the book and let me — "

All too aware of the spot where his fingers had made contact with the inch of bared skin at her waist and realizing protests were quite useless, she surrendered the book, tucked her blouse hastily back into the waistband of her gathered jersey skirt and watched as Dominic climbed the step stool and placed the book in the appropriate spot on the shelf. She couldn't help but notice how the muscles of his back and shoulders shifted beneath the fine fabric of his shirt, the way his tailored black pants clung to his thighs.

"Thanks," she said reluctantly when he'd lithely returned to the floor and stood facing her. "There are moments when I wish I were a little taller."

"You're perfect as you are. I wouldn't change a thing."

She was aware suddenly that his voice was the only sound in the shop. Everyone else seemed to have stopped whatever they were doing in order to listen. Nancy, at the cash register, ringing up a purchase for Edna Johnson; a pair of teenagers in the process of picking up the latest bestselling paperbacks from the display near the front counter; a stout middle-aged man just on his way out the door with a clutch of mystery novels in his hand. And the whole damn bunch of them were looking expectantly in Jane's direction.

Jane coughed in embarrassment, which seemed to be the cue for everyone to return to their own business. "Mr, er, Dom, what can I do for you?" Jane's voice had dropped almost to a whisper.

"You can," he whispered back, "stop being so prickly and let me take you out to dinner. I want to talk to you about Dee, about the trip to Mexico. She told me today, during our shoot, that the trip is up to you."

"And you thought taking me out to dinner would butter me up, make sure

I come out on Deirdre's side — on your side," Jane hissed. "Well, put your wallet away. I don't need to be buttered. I've already made up my mind. I do intend to go. So — ," her eyes shone with the perverse pleasure at bringing him down a peg, " — your coming here has been quite wasted."

"I disagree, Jane. I admit that trying to persuade you to go to Mexico was one of my motives, but not the only one." He hesitated, and Jane wondered for a moment if he was going to lie and say he had a craving for her company. "I seem to recall," he said, "that you wanted to talk to me about your niece. About, er, hanky-panky." He grinned as Jane blushed. "I'm offering you a chance to do that now, and I'm throwing dinner into the bargain. How can you resist?"

Earlier that afternoon Jane had decided she would go to Mexico. She'd checked out her finances, then asked Nancy how she felt about minding the store in her absence. Nancy was more than happy to oblige; the experience, she said, would be good for her, and she also thought her boss could use a holiday. Jane's last remaining qualms about the trip centred on the man who stood before her now. It appeared she could put her mind at rest in that department, too.

"You're right," Jane said after a moment. "I can't resist."

She immediately regretted putting her reply that way. She should have known better than to give Dominic any chance to tease. But apparently willing to give her a break, he only smiled, that devastating smile, and said quietly, "I've got a cab waiting outside. I'll just put myself on a holding pattern until you're finished here at the shop — unless you want to go home and change?"

His tone seemed to suggest that would be a good idea. Lord, why was it the men in her life were never happy about the way she dressed? Jane thought, and then immediately wondered how she could put a man like Dom in the same category as Fred. Feeling contrary, she said, "No. I don't exactly consider this dinner a date — " Jane was pleased to note a slight narrowing of Dom's eyes, " — so I think what I'm wearing will do. I'll be with you in five minutes."

Despite her denial that this was any sort of special occasion, Jane dashed into the washroom behind the shop, splashed her face with water, pulled a brush through the tangles of her hair, and fished in her bag for a tube of lipstick. As she outlined her full lips with pale coral, she suddenly stopped. What on earth was she doing? Was she actually hoping to beguile Dominic with her feminine charms? With a snort of disgust she dropped the tube back into her bag and wiped her lips with a tissue. Then she returned to the shop to help Nancy ring up the day's totals.

"Hey," Nancy said, "go on, get out of here. I saw that gorgeous hunk, and

I don't think you should waste any time. I can close up." She paused a moment, then added, "I know he's not your type, but gosh, is Fred gonna be jealous!"

"Nancy, please!" Jane protested. "It's not what you think. I'm just going out with the guy to talk about my niece — he's the photographer going on the shoot I told you about, the one Deirdre's mom wants me to — "

"Yeah, yeah, I gotcha, Jane. Too bad he's so hard on the eyes."

"Oh, shush!" Jane said, smiling.

She was still smiling as she left the shop, and failed at first to notice Dominic leaning against a nearby telephone pole. The look on his face when she did spot him was one of . . . what? Surprise? Her forehead creased momentarily in puzzlement, but before she had a chance to wonder further, he'd crossed to her, grasped her elbow and guided her into the cab running at the kerb.

"I know a little Indonesian place

uptown. Quiet enough for talking, but busy enough to indicate the food's good. And it really is. It's pretty spicy, though . . . " He turned his head to look more fully at her in the confines of the cab. "You like spicy food, don't you?"

Did this man take everything for granted? Jane wondered. What if she said she hated spicy food? Would he take her someplace she chose no matter how bland and pedestrian? Somehow she doubted it.

"As it happens," she said, stifling her continuing desire to be contrary, "I love spicy food. Especially Indonesian. Satay, with peanut sauce, is my favourite."

"Mine, too. Looks like we have something else in common."

Else? What else could they possibly have in common? Jane wondered. She decided he was just being polite. Trying to make her feel more at ease. Which was surprising, for in all of their past encounters, he'd seemed to take great delight in making her feel uncomfortable.

She sat back and neither of them spoke again until they were seated in the restaurant. When the waiter came to take their order for drinks, Dom suggested she might like to try the imported Indonesian beer.

"I usually drink white wine," Jane began.

"Try a beer. Just this once," Dom said good-naturedly. "It's perfect with spicy food."

"I . . . oh, all right." Jane nodded and her mouth turned up in a smile. "I'm game. I think it's a good idea to try to break old habits."

"Atta girl. I knew you had a sense of adventure."

"Does ordering beer qualify as adventure?"

"Believe me," he said, "for a lot of women it does."

Models, thought Jane with a peculiar twist in her midsection. *His* type.

After the waiter left their table,

Dominic said, "So. Let's talk about Dee." At her nod, he added, "And let's talk about her job in Mexico, even though you've already decided to go." He paused. "You see? Further proof that you're adventurous."

Jane couldn't suppress another smile, and seemingly encouraged, he went on, "I'd be a liar if I said my desire for your niece to go is purely in her interest."

The waiter returned with their beer, which he poured into two tall glasses, and so Jane had a moment to digest his comment. She took a sip of the brew and found it pleasantly sweet. "Whose interest then?"

"Mine."

She glanced up sharply. Was he saying that Deirdre meant something to him? Something that no other model did?

"Don't look so worried, Jane. I know what you're thinking, so let me put you straight. I am very interested in Dee, but in an entirely professional sense."

Taking Jane's lack of response as

a cue to carry on, he said, "It's models like Dee who've made me what I am. I've been called a brilliant photographer, and of course who wouldn't love being called brilliant?"

He quirked his mouth in a sort of self-effacing smile that Jane found totally disarming. She would never have guessed he could be this way. Still reluctant to let Dom think that anything about him met with her approval, she said dryly, "Lucky you."

She saw immediately that she had offended him. "Forgive me," she said, regretting her sarcasm, especially as he was so obviously making an effort to be friends. "I didn't mean that. Please, go on. I'm learning something."

He nodded. "You see, I firmly believe it's been my luck with working with the best models that's given me that reputation. Despite her relative inexperience, Dee is one of the best. And if she goes to Mexico for this shoot, she makes me look good. I make *her* look good, too, so together we create a kind of synergy, an energy that results in something greater than the sum of its parts. Make sense?"

Jane nodded. "Yes, it does. I understand exactly what you mean." When she had worked for a book publisher, she had seen that kind of thing sometimes between an author and editor. It was also, she thought, what had made her parents' marriage so rich. Synergy could happen with any relationship, she realized, romantic ones included, and when it did . . . Jane felt a little jolt go through her. It was what she'd foolishly hoped had been the case with her and Charles.

Dom must have seen the look of pain flash across her features. He studied her for a moment, and when he spoke, his voice was gentle. "I've said something to disturb you, haven't I?"

"No, no, it's nothing," she replied. "Just a memory I'd rather forget." She laughed self-consciously.

"Yes," he said, and the look on his

face was rueful. "I guess we all have those."

Did he really? Jane wondered. Or was he just making sympathetic noises?

When they'd ordered coffee, the conversation took a more personal turn. Jane lifted her gaze to Dom's, ignoring the charge that just looking into his eyes sent through her, and asked, "What made you decide to become a fashion photographer?"

He shrugged. "It was inevitable. My father was a journalist, and he wanted me to follow in his footsteps. But when my parents gave me a camera for Christmas the year I turned twelve, I got hooked on taking pictures. I still took journalism in college, among other things, and I thought maybe I'd be a photojournalist. I had a girlfriend in college who wanted to be a model, so I took pictures of her — lots of them — and, well, it seemed I had a talent for that. Things just went on from there."

"You found you'd rather just take

pictures of girls than, uh, more important subjects?"

Darn, she was doing it again. Allowing a note of disdain to enter her voice, and destroying the good feelings that were being established between them. What on earth was wrong with her?

Dom's face darkened. "I make no apology, Jane, for liking to photograph beautiful women. And who's to say what's important? Good photography, fashion photography included, makes people *feel* something, whether it's fear or awe, or sadness or delight. With the right models, good sets and lighting, I can create special auras, convey messages. My profession is commercial, no question, but it's creative, too, not to mention extremely lucrative. I also happen to love it."

"I'm sorry. I didn't mean to imply — "

"Yes, you did, Jane. But perhaps I can persuade you to come to a shoot and watch what happens. You saw the tail end of one last week,

93

but I think your mind was on other things . . . " His expression cleared and became wryly humorous.

Jane grinned, thinking, had anyone asked her a few days ago, she'd never have believed she would find anything funny about the night they'd hunted for Deirdre. "Yes, it was. And I wanted to thank you for helping me locate her. It was . . . kind of you."

She never would have believed she'd have thought of Dom as kind, either.

"You can repay me by coming to a shoot. Maybe sometime in the next few days?"

"Oh. I don't know. I'll see." Jane was flummoxed. Was he asking to see her again? No, not really. He simply wanted her to understand what he was about. It was his ego speaking. But why did he care what she thought about him?

Dominic interrupted her thoughts to ask if she wanted more coffee. At her hesitation, he said, "I do. Do you mind? Besides, I want to hear about you. I've been doing all the talking."

She found herself quite willing to reveal pieces of her past to him. She told him how she felt about the loss of her parents — with which he could sympathize, having lost his father four years earlier — what it was like coming to New York on her own, getting her first job, then the Book Nook, and finally how her older sister seemed to have it all — "looks included," Jane added ruefully.

Dominic frowned. "What do you mean? There's nothing wrong with the way you look."

Jane had always known that Sharon was the Cathcart girl who'd got the looks — slender height, thick straight blonde hair, a classically pretty face — and she accepted that. She, Jane, the 'little dark one', had got the brains.

"Thank you," she returned, "but you don't have to say that. I don't have a hang-up about my appearance." Dom looked as if he didn't quite believe her, but Jane ignored his reaction. She shook her head. "Good old Sharon. She's always badgering me to get out of New York, settle down with a 'nice guy' and start a family before my lungs collapse from the polluted air and my ovaries atrophy from disuse."

Dom laughed in genuine amusement. "Tell her there are more men in New York than anywhere else in the United States, so many in fact it's hard to make up your mind. Tell her you've taken a course in shallow breathing, so no problem with the polluted air."

Jane was laughing now, too, and she realized with surprise that she hadn't enjoyed dinner with someone so much in a long time. Someone to whom she enjoyed listening and who made her feel she was worth listening to in return. Why wasn't it quite the same with Fred? Dining out with him was pleasant of course, but dining out with Dominic had a certain undefinable edge. She paid no attention to the niggling voice in her head that reminded her Dom was virtually a professional woman charmer;

by the end of the meal, after a couple of beers — or was it three — the voice had disappeared altogether. She knew only that she'd enjoyed dinner and his company, and she was fully reassured that there was nothing between Deirdre and him beyond professional respect. At least on his part.

It was almost 9.30 by the time Dom took her home in a cab. Jane wondered if she should ask him to come in for coffee, then thought, no. Deirdre would be home soon, and who knew how she'd react to Dom's presence. Besides, she had to call Sharon and tell her it was all systems go for Mexico.

But when Dominic told the cabbie to wait, her worry about whether or not to ask him up to her apartment became academic. Jane wasn't sure if she was pleased or displeased. The beer, she decided, had definitely fuzzed her thinking.

He was surprisingly courteous. He insisted on accompanying her up the stairs to her apartment, and when she fumbled in her bag and eventually found her key, he took it from her hand and inserted it neatly in the lock, then opened the door and gestured for her to enter. He followed to stand just inside the doorway.

"Well," he said, "I've got an early shoot tomorrow, so I'll say good night — ah, lovely cat." Seymour had come up and begun rubbing against his leg, purring like a mad thing. "He acts like he's starved for love — but I suspect it's dinner."

Jane chuckled. "You bet. Obviously you know cats. Some of us eat to live, but they live to eat." She watched as Dom crouched to stroke Seymour. She saw the gentleness of his strong bronzed hands, how confidently they glided over the soft coat, his fingers, with their blunt tips and clean, square-cut nails, curling into and massaging the skin about the cat's neck. She could imagine those same hands, those same sensuous fingers, on her own skin, soothing, then exciting. She could see herself responding, her face like the ecstatic face of the heroine on a cover of one of Edna Johnson's historical romances . . .

She inhaled sharply, audibly, appalled at the direction of her thoughts. Dom looked up at her, and his eyes seemed lit from within. Had he read her mind? Had he guessed? *Oh, please, don't let him know*, she prayed.

She forced her expression into one of self possession. She straightened her shoulders, smiled politely and extended her hand. "Thank you, Dom, for dinner, and for putting my mind at rest about Deirdre. I'm grateful."

His face, too, suddenly changed. Gone was any trace of its former warmth and humour. In its place was a distant coolness, and as he grasped her hand briefly, he said in a voice as remote as his expression, as though the evening had never been, "You're quite welcome, Jane. Always glad to put a lady's mind at ease. Good-night."

Jane listened to his firm footfalls as

he descended the stairs, heard the faint opening and shutting of the main entry door, then the far-off sound of the cab door closing, the rev of the engine, then the sound receding as the cab sped off into the night.

She stood motionless for several minutes, her mind in turmoil. What had taken place that evening was far more than merely a reassurance that Deirdre's virtue was safe from a predatory photographer. Something had happened between her and Dominic, she was sure of it, and suddenly she was again having second thoughts about going to Mexico — but now for a completely different reason. It wasn't Deirdre she feared for. It was herself.

★ ★ ★

"Jane, is it okay? Are you gonna go? Are you?"

"Yup, let's dig out our sombreros."

Deirdre twirled about the room, her joy too great to be contained. Jane grinned at her. Deirdre was a great kid — most of the time. Jane had called Sharon only minutes before, after having convinced herself that her worries about being in the same orbit as Dominic Slater were unfounded. She put all thoughts of the earlier dinner down where they belonged — locked securely in a recessed corner of her heart and mind, not to be reopened. She'd given herself a stern talking to after Dom had left, realized the foolishness of letting a pleasant dinner and conversation carry her into fantasyland. For that was what her thoughts had been. Fantasy. Nothing more, nothing less. To think that Dom had felt anything like she had was utter nonsense.

Deirdre ceased her flurry of motion. "Oh, I can hardly wait. Just a week and a half from now — hey, not even that — we'll be in Mexico. And I'll be with Dom! Isn't that great?"

Oh, Deirdre, Jane thought, once again her heart breaking a little for her niece. Perhaps youth had more resilience than the more mature, but the pain of rejection that could be felt by a girl of fifteen-going-on-sixteen was just as intense as a woman of thirty would feel. Perhaps the heart bounced back to normal sooner, but try telling that to an inexperienced girl. No matter what pat phrases of comfort anyone gave you — like time heals all wounds — she wouldn't believe them.

Suddenly Deirdre sobered and said suspiciously, "Mom doesn't insist that you and I share a room, does she?"

"Deirdre, I'm hurt! You sound horrified at the idea of sharing a room with me. Gosh, and here I was thinking you liked sharing my apartment!" Jane declared with mock indignation.

But Deirdre didn't hear the teasing in her aunt's voice, and her face fell. "You mean we *are* sharing a room?"

Jane shook her head and smiled. "No, sweetie. You get to mess up one all by yourself."

The look on Deirdre's face made Jane think of the cat who'd got the cream. She shrank from the reason why Deirdre should be so pleased, but it was inescapable. Over the past few days, Jane had pieced together the fact that her niece seemed to see Jane as a threat to the course of true love, and maybe — horrors! — even as feminine competition for his affection. Deirdre's fear that her aunt was some sort of competition would also account for her recent enthusiasm for Fred, and also her frequent little mentions of how Dominic really liked tall women, not small ones like Jane — 'even though,' she would always add, 'there are lots of guys who like your type'.

Jane was getting thoroughly tired of hearing about her type.

Then Deirdre came up with a new inspiration. "Hey, Jane!" she said brightly. "Why don't you get Fred to go, too? Then you'll have someone to do stuff with . . . "

"Uh, nice thought, Deirdre, but I

really don't think so. Fred and I are good friends and all that, but . . . "

She hesitated. Should she explain to Deirdre about the way things were with Fred — and why? No, she decided. She wasn't sure her niece would understand. "Fred is too busy at work these days," she said. "And besides, I'm quite good at entertaining myself."

She meant it. She'd have no problem finding her own way about in the Yucatan, seeing the Mayan ruins, relaxing on the beach, reading books, writing letters, all the things people on vacation did. That would be enough. And she would avoid Dom. She knew only too well about the fragility of the heart, and she was not about to put hers to the test again.

★ ★ ★

"You're what? You're going where? In August? Are you out of your mind?"

Jane and Fred were sitting at a small table in a deli not far from the Book

Nook. "Shhh, Fred. Calm down. It's not that big a deal."

Fred lowered his voice. "I hate this idea of your going south during the hottest season of the year," he said. "And all because that niece of yours needs a baby-sitter and her own parents seem perfectly willing to dump that responsibility on you."

Jane knew that the arguments Fred made for why she was a fool for taking the trip were valid, but she suspected they were not the major reasons he was so opposed. She hadn't left out the detail that Dominic Slater would also be going. She hadn't forgotten the way Fred had reacted to him when they'd met.

She suddenly saw a way to make him feel a little less left out — as she was certain he was feeling. "Fred, would you mind feeding Seymour while I'm gone? I'll give you a key, and if you could just drop in once a day and give him some food, scoop out his litter every other day or so . . . "

"Of course. No problem," Fred said, a look of pleasure suffusing his face.

The reason for his happy acquiescence, despite the fact he and Seymour were hardly friends, struck Jane. He was interpreting her request as a desire to move their relationship on to another, more intimate plateau; her giving him a key to her apartment for whatever reason was in effect giving him a key to her heart. This, of course, had not been Jane's intent, but the moment she recognized what she had done, she felt a surge of guilt. She shouldn't be using Fred this way, shouldn't let him think that her request was a step toward a closer relationship. Oh, well. Too late now.

* * *

"So you *are* going to Mexico. Oh, Jane, that's super. And like I told you before, no problem for me to hold the fort here in the Nook. You need a break."

"Thanks, Nance. You're the best."

"Hey, what about your cat? Do you want me to feed him?"

Jane fervently wished she'd spoken to her shop assistant before Fred. But the damage was done. "No, it's okay. Fred's going to drop in every day and feed the big guy. Seymour will maybe be starved for affection but at least not for Little Vittles for Kittles."

"Where do they get those names?" Nancy laughed. "Well, tell Fred if he ever finds he can't get over to your place, I'll be glad to fill in. When are you leaving? A week from Monday, you said?" Nancy paused a moment and gave her boss a probing look. "Hmmm, and you said that handsome photographer is going, too, didn't you?"

Jane felt herself colour. "Nancy, will you give me a break? Yes, you know he's going, but he's certainly not the reason *I'm* going — I told you about my sister insisting — "

"Right," said Nancy. "I know how it is with you and Fred. I don't want you to worry about a thing while you're away. Between Fred and me the home front'll get good care."

Jane smiled gratefully. The phone rang, and while Nancy answered it, Jane headed for the box of just-released books that had come in that morning from the wholesaler. "Jane, it's for you," called Nancy. Jane turned and noted the interested look on her assistant's face. She snatched up the receiver. "Hello?"

She recognized the voice immediately. It was Dom. "Jane, I've looked at my schedule, and I've got a shoot coming up where an extra person on the set won't cause a problem."

What was he talking about? And then Jane remembered. He had mentioned the night before that she might like to watch a shoot, but she hadn't thought he'd really meant it. An odd sensation rippled through her, sort of what you'd feel standing on the edge of a cliff looking down at the churning water below.

"Uh, when?" she said, almost hoping that the time he gave her would be impossible for her to manage. And if not, maybe she could think of some excuse.

"Tomorrow morning. I'll be working with a really experienced model, and she has no problem with strangers on the set. It's a shoot I think you'll find enlightening."

Jane wanted to say no, but instead she found herself blurting, "All right. I can make it. Nancy can handle the shop — " she glanced at Nancy who nodded vigorously " — and . . . uh, what time exactly?"

"Come about eleven. Then we can have some lunch together, too."

"Oh. I'm not sure about lunch, but . . . "

Nancy reached over to give her a sharp poke in the ribs, her head again nodding vigorously. "Well, I'll see. But I'll be there at eleven."

She hung up the phone, stunned by her ready agreement to Dom's suggestion. She turned quickly to her assistant. "Nance, I appreciate your willingness to look after this place alone, but I'm going to be away for a whole week, and I think that's quite enough of a sacrifice for you to make, without my destroying your lunch-hours, too!"

"Jane, stop it, it's okay. So. Was that the gorgeous hunk who was in here yesterday?" She caught the blush that stained Jane's cheeks and said, "Uh-huh, thought so. And you know what? I won't say a word to Fred."

"Nancy! It's not like that. I'm just going to observe a photography session, that's all."

"Yeah, and have a little lunch." As she spoke, Nancy moved off toward the back of the shop, but Jane could still hear her chuckle. Drat, this was all she needed.

Then she was struck by something else. If Nancy was so sure there was some sort of romance brewing between her and Dom, why was she so offhand about it? Offhand, too, about Fred's feelings? Fred, whom she liked and respected?

After a moment Jane chalked up Nancy's attitude to the fact that Nancy just enjoyed teasing her. She didn't really believe there was anything going on between her boss and the photographer. For, anyone who knew Jane would know that a man like Dominic Slater was not her type.

6

JANE sat transfixed. The room was a study in stark contrasts. Globes of light and pockets of shadow. White props against a black backdrop. A sylph-like model was moving rhythmically to a hypnotic blend of drums and pulsing guitar, her skin a luminous white, her body wrapped in pieces of shiny black leather, a wealth of burnished gold jewellery flashing at her neck and wrists. She flung back her head, arching her swan-like neck, then dropped it to her chest, silken strands of her white-blonde hair falling forward wantonly. Her arms swept forward and back, as her swirling, twisting body seemed to obey commands from within and without.

"Perfect, Monique, perfect," Dominic said, shifting agilely from one spot to another, his hand-held camera fixed on its subject. His voice was deep, cajoling, then soothing and sensual — like a lover's, thought Jane. And his words, also like a lover's, "Yes, sweetheart, yes, beautiful. Yes, that's it, *feel* it . . . "

After a while, Jane heard Dominic say, his voice now calm, matter-of-fact, "Okay, we've got it." He lowered his camera, and strode over to his model. "You were fantastic, Monique." He dropped a brief kiss on her mouth.

Monique breathed deeply, then stepped back and smiled radiantly. "I *felt* fantastic, Dom. You always bring out the best in me." Then, hips swaying, she headed for the small dressing-room just off to one side of the studio.

"Wow," Jane said when Dom came over to her. "That was really . . . something." She fought a crazy stirring of jealousy.

He smiled. "Come on. Let's go have some lunch. I'm starving. I hope you don't mind, but I took the liberty of ordering food in for lunch. Restaurants around here on a Saturday noon are jammed, and since it's so hot outside I thought you might appreciate staying out of the heat."

The upstairs apartment was furnished like the man. Masculine. Strong. And just a little intimidating. A black leather sofa sat along one wall faced by a matching chair and ebony coffee-table. The carpet was a dense deep red. An entire wall was lined with books, and the other walls bore framed photographs, some black and white, some colour. Jane itched to take a closer look at them, but Dom took her by the arm and led her to the far end of the room, to a dining-table of inlaid oak, a work of art in itself.

"Sit," he commanded, holding out one of the elegant chairs. "You can look at my etchings after we eat. I'll just go into the kitchen and throw together our gourmet treat." He laughed at her inquiring look and explained, "I have to take it out of the little cardboard cartons and put it on some decent plates. Be right back. Don't move."

Within minutes Dom was seated cornerwise to her at the table and they were munching warm and tasty croissant sandwiches and a delicious julienne salad.

Between mouthfuls, Dom said, "Now you may tell me what you thought of the shoot. Something beyond 'wow', I mean." He grinned to take the edge off his gibe.

"At first I didn't know what to think," she answered honestly. "But after a while I could almost . . . feel the current between you and Monique. I understand what you were saying the other night about synergy. And it was almost a — " Jane hesitated, then plunged on " — a seduction. I mean, the camera seducing its subject, to make her bend to . . . its will." His will, she meant.

"But you realize it was all an act, don't you? A way to help the model play her role convincingly."

"Of course!" Jane said too quickly. Intellectually, she understood. But emotionally, how she felt about the shoot, while it was in progress and afterward, was another matter.

Dom had poured them each half a glass of white wine, and Jane had been sipping at hers judiciously. Now her glass was empty, and Dom reached for the bottle sitting in a cooler between them.

"Oh, I really shouldn't have any more . . . " she murmured. She glanced at him, and the amused look in his eyes made her change her mind. She hated being predictable. "Well, what the heck, a little won't hurt," she said. She also wanted suddenly to restore the easy camaraderie of the other night. "But I do have to work this afternoon, you know, and Nancy would never forgive me if I stumbled in drunk."

He grinned. "Why? Do you often stumble in drunk?"

"Well, I try not to make a habit of it."

"That's a relief. Drunken women are not my favourite."

She took a bite of sandwich. "What is your favourite?"

"Sweet biddable things who don't ask personal questions with their mouths full of tunafish."

She swallowed, then reached for her wine and sipped it. "Sorry. I don't usually do that," she said. "Ask personal questions, I mean." She laughed, then added, "I don't usually talk with my mouth full, either."

"Jane, I can see you're a woman of class." He forked some more salad onto her plate, then his own. "But come — let's just eat and enjoy."

How neatly he'd sidestepped her question, Jane thought.

When at last they had polished off most of the food — and the wine, Jane noticed — Dom said, "I guess you want to get back to the shop. I trust you're not inebriated?"

Jane smiled. It had been a delightful, if not entirely relaxing lunch, and she was sorry it had to end. "I think I'm sober enough to manage," she replied lightly. "But first I'd love a closer look at some of those photographs on your walls. May I?"

"Of course."

She got up and wandered over to one that particularly caught her eye. It was a colour photo and reminded Jane of impressionist art; the image was unfocused, soft, ethereal. A sweet-faced young woman, her golden hair tumbling childlike over her shoulders, was sitting on a small stone bench in what looked like an English garden in spring. She was gazing in gentle awe at a pink rose in her hand, as if it were a wondrous gift from . . . what? A lover.

"Ah, yes. One of my favourites. It was one of a series of perfume ads."

"It's exquisite. Who's the model? She looks a bit like Deirdre."

There was a moment of silence before Dom replied tersely, "My ex-wife."

Ah, of course. Though Katya looked

different in every picture, Jane should have recognized her, should have guessed. She shot him a glance, but it was as though a veil had been dropped over his face. *Don't lift it*, a voice inside Jane said.

Dominic placed a hand on Jane's shoulder, turning her around till she faced him fully. "I guess I'd better send you on your way. Jane, I — "

He stopped speaking abruptly. Jane could feel his warm breath on her face, and her body could feel the heat of his. When, lips parted slightly, he lowered his head, Jane thought nothing had ever been more inevitable.

She didn't even think to protest. The instant his mouth made contact, any will she possessed vanished. She found herself surrendering utterly to the swift surge of passion, powerless to fight it. The kiss went on and on, spiralling her downward into depths of feeling she'd forgotten could exist. Her arms came round to embrace him, her hands clinging hard to the smooth, firm contours of his back. He cupped her face with his palms as if to make her mouth even more accessible, more one with his. She could feel an incredible burning on her lips, on her cheeks, throughout her whole being.

And then, all too soon, his mouth left hers. His hands fell to his sides, and he stepped away. "I think, Jane," he said somewhat raggedly, "that you'd better leave — before I won't let you leave."

"Yes, you're right," she murmured in confusion. "I must get back to the shop."

Dominic led her to his door, down the staircase, and out the front door. Despite the blast of heat, Jane felt oddly chilled as she watched Dom hail a passing cab. It stopped, and he urged Jane into it. They each murmured a strangely polite good-bye and thank you, and then he closed the cab door. She looked through the window to watch him as he turned and headed back up the walk to his house. Her overwhelming feeling was regret. How could she have let that kiss happen? Why hadn't she been the one to stop it? Did he, too, suffer regrets?

"Where to, lady?"

"Pardon?"

"Where do you want to go?" barked the impatient cabbie. "Or do you just want to spend the afternoon sitting here at the kerb?"

"Oh, no, of course not," she managed, then gave him the address of her shop.

By the time the cab pulled up in front of the shop, Jane had regrouped. But while her exterior looked composed, inside she was a mess.

She wasn't ready for what awaited her in the shop. An angry Deirdre who launched herself at Jane the moment she walked through the door.

"Jane!" she shrilled, causing heads to swivel in their direction. "Why didn't you tell me you were seeing Dom? How could you do this to me?"

"Deirdre — "

But her niece wasn't interested in what Jane might have said. Throwing her aunt a look of fury, she pushed by her and practically ran out the door. Jane could only watch in helpless misery.

Nancy walked over to her and said, "Geez, Jane, I'm sorry. But when Deirdre came in here a few minutes ago looking for you, I told her where you were. Should I have kept my mouth shut?"

"No. Yes. I mean, it's fine. There's no reason in the world you shouldn't have told her where I was. None at all."

But even as she spoke, Jane knew it was a lie. The same reason Nancy shouldn't have said anything to Deirdre was the same reason Jane herself hadn't. The same reason she hadn't mentioned she'd had dinner with him the other night — that Deirdre *would* see her as competition for Dominic's affections.

Jane sighed. "I'll straighten out Deirdre's misunderstanding tonight when I get home. She has a tendency to blow everything out of proportion. She has this silly crush on Dominic, you see, and I think she thinks . . . ”

“Say no more,” Nancy said, nodding in understanding. “I get the picture.” She paused and her look was speculative. “But you say there’s nothing going on between you and this photographer, right? I know I’ve been teasing you, but I also know that you’ve got a solid relationship with Fred. That you couldn’t possibly have anything in common with a guy who takes pictures of models for a living. And Deirdre’s just a kid, isn’t she? And kids overreact.”

“Thanks, Nancy. You’ve hit the nail right on the head.”

But she hadn’t, not really. Yes, Deirdre was overreacting. Yes, Jane valued Fred. And yes, Dominic and she did not have a lot in common. But she found herself wanting to defend what he did for a living, explain to Nancy that fashion photography wasn’t as frivolous as it appeared. And as for her solid relationship with Fred, well, why were her lips still burning from another man's kiss? Why did her body still feel the pressing heat of his? She remembered how the moment had seemed to go on and on, how she'd wanted it never to end . . .

★ ★ ★

Her confrontation with Deirdre later was not a pleasant one. When Jane opened the apartment door, she was met by an ominous silence. No rock and roll from the stereo, no off-key singing, no clatter of dishes from the kitchen. Her first thought was that Deirdre was out and up to Lord only knew what. But a glance across the room revealed her niece wedged silent and unmoving in a corner of the sofa, her face in a mutinous pout, her gaze fixed on Jane.

There was no point putting off the inevitable, so Jane dove right in.

"Deirdre, I know you're angry at me, but you mustn't be." At her niece's scoffing huff, Jane rushed on, "If you think there is something going on between Dominic Slater and myself, think again. There is nothing, I repeat, nothing between us."

Despite the kiss, she believed that was true. *She* might be feeling something for Dom, but he could not possibly feel anything much for her. A kiss meant nothing to such a man. If she were foolish enough to entertain any thoughts to the contrary, then she would only be setting herself up for certain heartbreak. For there was no way in the world Dominic could look upon her as anything other than a temporary diversion. And even in the unlikely event that he did, Jane would have to put a check on her emotions and steer clear. He could be a clone of Charles Dunlevy. An attractive, charismatic man in the kind of glamorous profession that seemed to land beautiful women constantly at his doorstep, which in Dominic's profession was the literal truth.

Jane knew that she might be seen as sweet, intelligent, maybe even attractive, but there was no way she could compete. Furthermore, she didn't want to.

She looked at her niece and added, "He simply invited me to watch a shoot, no more no less."

"Liar! Nancy told me you had lunch with him, too! And why would he ask you to come to a shoot? And why not one I was doing?"

The betrayal she saw in her niece's face, and the sickening realization that she had, in fact, lied — by omission, perhaps, but still a lie — filled her with guilt. She realized maybe she should have told Deirdre, but it was just this very reaction she'd hoped, however foolishly, to avoid.

"Probably not one of your shoots," Jane said reasonably, "because you didn't have a session with him today or in the next few days. Dominic wanted me to watch a shoot as soon as possible, because he thought it would make me feel better about going to Mexico."

"But you'd already decided you were going," muttered Deirdre.

"I know, but I guess he just wanted to, er, cement that. Make me see just what a shoot with a model is really like."

"But why lunch? Was that part of the . . . cement?"

Why do I feel like I just got caught stealing the Crown Jewels? Jane asked herself crossly. But she said gently, "Deirdre, honey, we only had lunch because it seemed like a logical thing to do. We were both hungry and I think Dominic was just being polite. We had a quick bite, and all we talked about was his work — " suddenly Jane had a flash of inspiration — "and what a great model you are."

"You did?" Deirdre's expression changed from sulkiness to hopefulness, and Jane felt guiltier by the second.

"You really talked about me? What did he say?"

Jane recalled what he'd said two nights earlier over dinner. "That you're a natural. He says models like you make him look good. Sort of a magic."

"Gosh, did he really say that! See, Jane, I told you he loves me." At her aunt's abrupt elevation of her eyebrows, she rushed on, "That's just his way of saying it. He's too cool to come right out and tell it like it is, because he's — "

"Okay, okay, Deirdre." Jane was tired of trying to make the girl see the situation for what it was — on her side, a crush on a glamorous man; on his, professional respect for a good model.

Deirdre stood up and came over to her aunt. She smiled apologetically. "Oh, Jane, I'm sorry for thinking that way about you and Dom. I know you'd never steal another woman's man, and I also know you're not his type."

"Steal . . . ?" Jane shook her head

in despair. And if she heard that stuff about 'type' one more time, she'd be certifiable. She calmed herself, softened, and reached out to give her niece a hug. "You're right, Deirdre. Have no fear about Dominic and me ever becoming an item. Not a chance."

The flare-up of passion in his apartment only hours before again leapt to mind, but Jane crushed the memory. "Hey. I've got a great dinner for us tonight. One of your favourites — pasta with pesto sauce, and Caesar salad."

Deirdre brightened. "Yum. Can I make the croutons?"

★ ★ ★

They decided to leave for Mexico the following Saturday — in advance of everyone else, and two days before the shoot was scheduled to begin. It would give Deirdre a chance to acclimatize herself and rest up for the work to follow. Acquire a bit of a tan. A day and a half slathered with a medium-strength sunscreen should do the trick. And while Deirdre was busy carefully toasting her pale skin to the desired honey gold, Jane would go off and explore.

She could hardly wait. Even though Dominic, Joss and the others involved in the shoot would be staying at the same hotel — a luxurious beach front high rise with a number of 'neat, real romantic beach cabanas', so Deirdre had told Jane — they apparently wouldn't be around till late Sunday. So Jane was safe till then. And then, surely, Dominic would be so busy the chances of an encounter with him would be slight. She hoped.

The week prior to their departure was particularly hectic, because on the Tuesday morning before their departure, Seymour took it into his contrary feline brain to disappear.

He'd dashed out the apartment door just as Jane was leaving for work, raced down the stairs ahead of her and made good his escape as another tenant, unaware of the cat's presence, swung open the front door of the building. Seymour darted out on to the sidewalk and into a back alley. He was not an outdoor cat, and Jane was worried sick about him all day, for her efforts to retrieve her pet before she went to work were in vain. When she hurried home that evening, he still wasn't around. She and Deirdre roamed the streets till almost midnight calling his name.

"Why is Seymour doing this?" she wailed to her niece when, dispirited, they gave up the search for the night. "He hates the outdoors. The traffic scares him, there's no neat little box of litter for him to use, no waiting bowl of Kittle Vittles. I just don't understand it."

"Maybe," Deirdre said, "he knows you're gonna be leaving him next week, and this is his way of keeping you here. I've heard that cats do that kind of thing."

"I've heard that, too, but I never believed it. Now I'm not so sure. Seymour has never done anything like this before." She couldn't, just couldn't, go off to Mexico without knowing Seymour was home and safe.

The following evening after work, just as Jane was rounding the corner of her street, her glance darting constantly from side to side hoping to catch a glimpse of Seymour, she heard a jubilant, "Jane, we've found him!"

Jane looked up to see Deirdre standing in front of the apartment building, gleefully hugging the truant Seymour. And standing beside her was Dom. A Dom decidedly the worse for wear. His shirt had a jagged tear, his face bore a smudge of dirt, and his normally sleek hair was rumpled. She was glad that she was still far enough away for her gasp of surprise to go undetected. She hurried up to Deirdre, took the cat from her and buried her face in his fur, scolding him gently. After a moment she raised her head and her glance went from Dom to Deirdre and back to Dom.

"Why are you here?" she asked him. "And what happened to you? You look like you've been run over by a truck."

He ran a hand through his hair and glanced balefully at his torn shirt. "A truck might have been preferable to that damn alleyway," he said. "And I'm here because Dee told me today at our shoot that Seymour was missing, and you know me — " he smiled broadly at Jane " — I never miss a chance to play Sir Galahad."

Jane coloured. He'd helped her find Deirdre that night, yes. Was he also making some sort of oblique reference to his gallant withdrawal from a kiss that had promised to lead into dangerous territory?

"We finished early," Deirdre was saying, oblivious to any currents that may have passed between her aunt and her hero, "and so Dom offered to help in the search. He was fantastic! You should've seen him climb a fence and go into this nasty-looking back lane — you know the one over behind that row of shops on Fourth, where that body was found murdered last week?" Deirdre's eyes turned adoringly to Dom and then she threw her arms around his neck and gave him a smacking kiss on his cheek.

Dom looked embarrassed by her display. He gently unwound her arms from his neck and grinned self-consciously. "I just did what anyone would've done, Dee."

"Not any man, Dom. Only you!"

Jane studied his face and thought she saw a fleeting look of annoyance, but perhaps it was only her imagination. She knew one thing, though. Going to Mexico probably wasn't going to help Deirdre get over her crush. And it wasn't going to help her get over hers, either!

7

JANE and Deirdre took a cab from the Cancun airport to the Hotel d'Oro, on the sea about two miles from the town itself. Their driver, Jane learned to her delight, was Mayan. His English was good, and, proud of his heritage, he told an interested Jane that she must go to Tulum and Coba, a couple of excavated Mayan sites relatively near Cancun — or at least a not-too-expensive cabfare away, he said with a hopeful smile.

By the time Jane and Deirdre entered the lobby of their hotel, it was mid-afternoon, and there was lots of time for a swim. They hurried up to their respective rooms — Jane's on the tenth floor, Deirdre's on the twelfth — to change.

Jane's eyes nearly left their sockets when she met her niece at the pool ten minutes later. "What do you call that?" she asked as she stared in amazement at what Deirdre was wearing, or rather what she wasn't.

"It's a bathing suit," replied her niece, her blue eyes the picture of innocence.

"No. What *I'm* wearing is a bathing suit," Jane said, gesturing at her own modest one-piece lycra suit. "What you're wearing is illegal!"

Jane had seen tiny bikinis before, but this one was no more than a G-string, which left the wearer's derriere completely exposed, paired with a skimpy top that concealed only a minute portion of Deirdre's youthful breasts.

"Oh, Jane," protested Deirdre, "these are all the rage in Europe. Don't be so *provincial*. In fact at most beaches in Europe, some in the Caribbean, too, the women don't wear tops at all."

"How do you know that?" Jane asked, wondering, too, where her niece had picked up the term 'provincial'.

Deirdre groaned in exasperation. "*Everybody* knows that, Jane. Where have you been?"

Obviously only places where people wore clothes, Jane thought, and then remembered the male strip club. Well, usually. Aloud she said, "Let's grab a couple of loungers, Deirdre. Before all the men around this pool die of apoplexy."

When they were stretched out side by side, Deirdre explained, "I want to get as much of an all-over tan as I can, Jane. The clothes I'll be modelling all expose different parts of the body."

"Your, uh, cheeks, too?" Jane asked incredulously.

"No, silly, but some of the outfits might be cut really high in the leg and, well, this suit makes it so no one will think about tan lines, you know?"

Maybe not tan lines, Jane agreed silently, but they might think of one of two other things . . . She got up and lowered herself into the shallow end of the pool. Maybe she was just a silly old-fashioned maiden aunt after all.

"Don't forget to use some sunscreen," warned Jane.

"Don't worry. I won't. A sunburn is the last thing I need. Dom'd kill me." She flicked a strand of hair from her cheek and smiled as if there could be nothing more delightful than being murdered by Dom. "What are you going to do, Jane?" she asked. "Tromp around in this heat and look at boring old ruins, I suppose."

"You've got it. And they are *not* boring. Ruins represent the rise and fall of great civilizations."

Deirdre's only response was to roll her eyes.

★ ★ ★

"Stop! Thief!"

The small boy raced off through the crowd of shoppers in the outdoor Sunday morning market-place of Cancun, Jane's purse clutched under his arm. Jane gave chase, but within moments had lost sight of the pint-sized robber.

"Oh, no," she wailed. All her identification, traveller's cheques and one hundred American dollars were in her bag. Except for the cash, the contents were all replaceable, but the purse was not. It was her favourite, a worn leather shoulder-bag that had been a gift from her mother years ago. The boy had jostled her in the crowd of shoppers, the purse had fallen off her shoulder, and he'd made good his grab-and-run. This, she thought in dismay, was no way to start a holiday. Why hadn't she followed her original plan and hired a driver, or taken a bus straight to the Mayan ruins at Tulum, instead of stopping by the market in Cancun first?

As she began to head back toward the square, a small commotion broke out behind her. She turned, and her mouth fell open in surprise. Her small assailant had been captured and was being dragged her way.

His captor was Dominic.

"What . . . ? How . . . ?" Jane stammered, when the pair stood before her.

"He ran right into me," said Dominic, his eyes glittering angrily at the purse snatcher. He handed Jane her bag, then shifted the camera slung over his shoulder into a more comfortable position. "I didn't see him grab it, but I heard shouts of *thief*, so I figured this character — " he shook the boy's skinny brown arm " — was the culprit. Then a couple of shoppers pointed you out and, well, here we are."

"Thank you," Jane breathed, "thank you. I never expected to see my purse again. But what are you doing here? I thought you weren't coming till tonight."

"First let me deal with this young scrap." Dom said. He clasped the boy by both shoulders and leaned down to glare at him. *"Pide perdon a la señorita. Ahorita!"* he commanded.

Jane's feeble knowledge of Spanish

140

allowed her to recognize that Dominic had demanded an apology. The boy raised his head and turned enormous and fearful black eyes on Jane. "I . . . sorry, lady," he said. "English no very good."

Dominic smiled tightly and said to Jane, "Stay right here. And hang on to your bag. I'll be back."

And with that he marched the thief toward the square. Jane watched as they reached a bench, sat down and began to talk. After a minute, Dominic dug into a pocket of his stylish cotton pants and drew out what appeared to be a roll of bills. He peeled one off the top and handed it to the boy. They both stood, shook hands, then the boy took off down a side street. Dominic watched him go, then turned back toward Jane.

"What did you tell him?" Jane asked when he reached her side. "How come you're so fluent in Spanish? And did I see you giving him money? You gave money to a thief?"

"What is this? The Inquisition?" He grinned, and shook his head to stop the apology he could see forming on Jane's lips. "I really don't mind your questions. I know Spanish because my mother is Mexican. She taught me."

Ah, that explained his black hair and olive complexion too, Jane thought. She kept silent as Dominic went on, "Down here some thiefs aren't as bad as others. Some are helping to support their families — at least that was his story, and maybe I'm a sucker, but I believed him. So I gave him some money." He smiled resignedly. "But I also gave him a good talking to. Told him if I saw him sniffing around the town again, I'd paddle him so hard he wouldn't sit down for a week."

"Ha! You think that'd work? Wow. I never took you for a softie."

"Dig deep and you'll find that beneath this tough exterior, I'm just mush inside."

"So . . . how is it your mushy self is here?" Jane asked. "I thought you weren't coming to Cancun till tonight."

Despite her teasing words, Jane was thinking, yes, there was much about this man she had misread. Every time she was with him she learned something new.

"Most of the others are arriving later," he replied. "But I wanted to get here early so I could scout the sites. I just stopped in at the market to grab some fresh fruit. Now I'm after a cab."

"Well, I won't keep you any longer. But I wish there was something I could do in return."

"There is, as a matter of fact. You can come with me to Tulum."

Jane inhaled sharply. She wanted to say yes. She wanted to say no. She had planned to go to Tulum herself that afternoon, and here was a perfect opportunity. But what about her vow to avoid Dom? Her assurances to Deirdre?

At her hesitation, he said with feigned impatience, "Look, lady, you told me last week you wanted to see Mayan ruins, and here I am offering to take you along with me in my cab, and giving you a perfect way to pay me back for my chivalry to boot. You're dressed for it — " he paused to peruse her practical walking shorts, T-shirt and sneakers " — so what's your problem?"

You, Jane wanted to say. You, and your damned attractiveness, and the way I react to it. "None," she said. "Let's go."

A couple of hours later, they were standing outside the Temple of the Frescoes, looking up at the eroded limestone pillars and archway that gave entrance to the facade of the building. "Jane, do me a favour. Stand over there — " he gestured to a crumbling archway " — so I can take your picture."

"Please, no. I . . . look awful in pictures."

"How did I know you'd say that?" Dominic said, a note of humorous exasperation in his tone. "Jane, it doesn't matter if you come out looking like Godzilla, though I assure you that you won't. I just want to frame this spot, see what the afternoon light is like, try out a couple of filters. Consider yourself a prop, if you must."

"Thanks."

"A very pretty one."

Normally Jane would have been either embarrassed or annoyed by the compliment, but strangely she wasn't. Recognizing there was little point in being obstinate, she did as she was bid. Dominic took a few shots, then stopped. "Jane," he said. "Don't look directly at the camera. Look over there, and there — " he pointed " — and move a little."

Jane shifted self-consciously. "Dominic, I'm not one of your models! I can't do this. Besides, I thought you just wanted to 'frame' a picture."

"Yes, but there's no harm in making the focal point of the picture look good." At Jane's frown, he added,

"I'm sorry. Guess I'd better turn off the automatic pilot. I get behind a camera and . . . " He paused, and said, "But try this — think about . . . the man in your life. Think about being with him. How good it feels."

Obligingly Jane thought about Fred. But not much happened. A mild rush of affection perhaps, but no feelings of thwarted desire, no passion. Still, wanting to please Dominic for reasons she didn't want to examine, she allowed an expression of longing to cross her face.

It was surprisingly easy. The man she thought about was Dominic.

"Perfect," he said, and began snapping away. "You want him, you miss him, he means a lot to you. Ah, yes, lovely."

His voice was reassuring, hypnotic, and Jane found herself responding. She tilted her head this way and that, stood with fists firmly on her hips, then pushing carelessly at her hair. At one point she leaned negligently against a stone pillar and her expression, one of longing, mirrored her secret thoughts.

"Great," he said after several minutes. "I think I got some good ones." Then he added, "Lucky guy."

Jane said nothing.

Dominic put his camera back in its case, and then took her arm and led her into the temple. They crossed to a wall that was covered in what appeared to be ancient drawings.

"This mural," said Dominic, "depicts some of the Mayan deities. It's one of the few that's well preserved."

"How did you know about it?" Jane asked.

"I was here once. Years ago."

Jane thought she detected a note of regret, or sadness, in his tone, but when she glanced quickly at his face, she saw only a stony solemnity. He pointed to one of the paintings, a stylized and, to Jane's eye, grotesque figure, with monster-like features. "That's Ixchel," he said. "Goddess of the moon and medicine and childbirth. There's a shrine to her on the island of Cozumel not all that far from here, and the ancient Mayas used to make pilgrimages to it." He laughed mirthlessly. "I even made a pilgrimage to it myself once."

Jane wondered about the last comment, but was oddly reluctant to hear any more details. She asked instead, "How come you know so much about the Mayas?"

"I studied their civilization when I was in college."

"I thought you said you took journalism."

Dom turned to her. "I also took journalism. Despite what you think, Jane, I'm not a one-trick pony."

"No, I didn't mean that," she protested. "In fact I'm learning you have many sides . . . " She smiled at him, trying to ease the sudden tension her question seemed to have caused. "I'm just interested, that's all. In you . . . and the Mayan civilization," she added quickly.

"Come with me." He took her arm

and drew her out of the temple, guiding her over toward the Castillo, one of the larger structures, which overlooked the sea. They made their way around it and perched comfortably, if somewhat precariously, on a ledge.

Jane gasped at the loveliness of the view. "We're facing east, aren't we?" she said, gazing out at the vast expanse of water, which went from deep rich turquoise to pale crystal as it stretched toward the horizon. "Wouldn't it be great to sit here at dawn and watch the sun come up? I wonder if the Mayas did that."

"Hmm. I thought so," Dom said.

Puzzled, Jane twisted to look at him. "You thought what?"

He turned and placed a finger on the tip of her nose. "You, my dear, like to play the role of sane, practical Jane. But deep inside — " he paused and gave her nose a gentle flick " — you're a true romantic."

Jane rubbed her nose, thinking she'd never thought the appendage could be so sensitive. "How, my dear," she drawled back, wishing her cheeks weren't flooding with colour, "have you come to that conclusion?"

"In much the same way I concluded you have a sense of adventure."

Jane looked at him in astonishment. "I'm not drinking beer right now!"

He threw his head back and laughed. "Jane, you're delightful. And you *are* a romantic. It's the way you talk about the sun coming up, I guess."

"Ha!" she returned. "It's just that I like doing dull things like watching the sunrises. And when I'm not being dull, I'm the wicked witch of the west. Just ask Deirdre."

"Deirdre," he said, "obviously does not know her aunt well." He paused to watch her blush. "Maybe we — you and I — can come watch the dawn some morning. I want to see what the light is like. Interested?"

"Oh, yes," Jane answered without thinking. Drat. She shouldn't have said that. She wasn't supposed to be spending time in this man's company. She'd vowed not to.

Dominic didn't pursue the topic. A thoughtful note entered his voice as he said, "I sometimes think the Mayas sat here and watched as the Spanish conquerors sailed into their shores. They had no idea what awaited them. No idea that the ships they were watching were full of men who would destroy them . . . "

Jane turned eyes round with surprise toward him. He constantly said things she didn't expect. "But isn't the reason for the end of their civilization still a mystery?"

"Not entirely. There are a number of theories. And certainly by the time Tulum was even built — around the end of the fifteenth century — their culture was on the decline. The Spanish just put paid to it completely."

A moment passed, then Jane said, "It's sad, isn't it?"

He twisted his body so that he could face her fully. "Yes," he agreed. "It makes me realize that our civilization, too, will decline. Sometimes I think it must, but other times I think there may be hope. The Mayas' lasted about a thousand years — longer than any other. Like ours, their culture was quite sophisticated. Mathematics, written language, a calendar even more accurate than ours, and a wealth of art and architecture. They were an incredible people. There's still so much we don't know . . . "

He fell silent, and so did she, both enjoying the contemplative moment. Suddenly he said, "Jane?"

"Hmm?"

"Would you have dinner with me tonight?"

"Oh, I . . . " Jane had been about to say she would, but then realized she could not. And must not. "I can't," she said. "Deirdre's expecting me to eat with her tonight, but maybe you'd like to join both of us?" she added, knowing that the invitation had to be made. Wishing things were otherwise.

"I don't think so," he said slowly.

Finally they made their way back to the parking area outside the ramparts of Tulum and climbed into a cab. It was almost six o'clock when they arrived at the hotel, and Jane suddenly felt anxious. What would she say when Deirdre asked how her day went? Should she tell her about running into Dominic? About how they went to Tulum together? "Oh, it was just a coincidence," she could imagine herself saying. "He was going to Tulum, I was going to Tulum. It only made sense to share a cab. No big deal, really . . . "

Drat. Why did she have to feel so guilty?

In the end she didn't have to tell her niece anything. After thanking Dominic and bidding him a hasty "See you," to which he made no reply beyond a clipped 'right' before striding off in the other direction, she dashed up to Deirdre's room. At her knock came a faint "Come in — it's open," and she entered to find Deirdre lying on her

153

bed, stretched out on her stomach.

"Deirdre, what's wrong?" Jane asked, hurrying to the girl's side.

"Oh, nothing that an icepack on my backside won't cure," the girl mumbled. She reached behind her and gingerly lifted the back of her oversize T-shirt. The area in question was covered with a plastic bag filled with ice, which sat on top of a damp washcloth.

Jane gasped in dismay. "Deirdre, that blasted G-string! Didn't you use sunscreen?"

Deirdre twisted her head, so that her aunt could get the benefit of her baleful gaze. "Yes, everywhere but there. I don't know how I could've been so stupid, but when I was slathering the stuff on down by the pool all these guys were watching me, and I just couldn't let them see me put stuff there. So I didn't. And I didn't intend to lie on my stomach for very long."

"But — "

"I fell asleep!"

"You poor kid. What are we going to do about dinner? I guess you don't want to sit down anywhere — "

"I don't think I'll ever be able to sit down again!" Deirdre wailed miserably.

"We can order from room service, though, and you can sort of prop yourself up on your side — "

Deirdre groaned. "Jane, I don't feel like eating at all. Dominic and some of the others may have already arrived, and I don't think I can put on a good enough act for them. Especially Dominic. He'll be angry at me for being so stupid." She groaned again. "Look, I . . . I just want to lie here and try to go to sleep. I'll be better in the morning."

"Well, okay," Jane said reluctantly. As she walked down the hallway toward the elevator, she remembered Dominic's invitation. Was it still good? And surely he'd be having dinner with the others if they'd arrived. She wondered again why he'd asked her. Torn, she entered her own room and sat staring at the phone for a few minutes. At last she picked it up, dialled the front desk and asked for Dominic Slater's room.

"I'm sorry, *señorita*," said a pleasant female voice in accented English, "but *Señor* Slater is in a cabana, and the cabanas do not have telephones." She hesitated, then, "I can give you his cabana number, if you like?"

"Oh, no, it's all right," Jane said, chickening out. But then abruptly she changed her mind. "Yes, I would like the number. It's . . . ?"

"Seven," said the woman, and Jane hung up, wondering if she would do anything with the information.

Deirdre's description of the cabanas rang through her head — 'real romantic'. So, he was in one of those?

In the end, she showered quickly and changed into the same lemon-yellow dress, then took the elevator to the lobby and headed outside toward the cabana area.

Number Seven was strategically placed

for privacy. Fronted by palms and its own little garden of hibiscus, it was a cosy-looking, red-tiled-roof-and-stucco affair that was surrounded by tall hedges. Jane walked up to the wooden door and knocked.

There was no answer. Jane was appalled at how disappointed she felt. She had promised herself she was going to avoid the man while in Cancun, yet here she was seeking him out. And then when she wasn't successful, feeling unbearably hard done by. This had to stop, she lectured herself. Sure, they'd shared an interesting and compatible afternoon, but what did it mean? Nothing, she told herself, beyond a pleasant few hours in the company of someone with whom she shared a few — very few — interests.

She straightened her shoulders and directed her steps back to the hotel. She glanced into the bar area on the terrace and saw no sign of him. Should she look in the dining-room? She passed the entryway of the spacious room and saw most of the tables occupied by happy, chatting groups and couples. And way over in a far corner she saw Dominic. But he wasn't alone. Joss, another man and a couple of women she didn't recognize were sitting with him, and they appeared deep in discussion. Jane couldn't see herself joining them, nor could she see herself sitting at a table alone. For if Dom saw her, which he undoubtedly would, he'd feel he'd have to ask her to join them and then . . .

It was all too much for Jane, so she decided on room service. She had the latest novel by one of her favourite authors to dig into, and she could spend the evening reading.

By nine o'clock, Jane was restless. Dinner had been tasty, but it was gone now, and the novel no longer held her interest. She walked out on to the balcony of her room and gazed out toward the beach. The night was warm, but there was a pleasant breeze, which stirred the light fabric of her dress. A good night for a stroll.

When she reached the sand she removed her sandals, then with them dangling from her hand made her way slowly down the beach till she was well past the hotel frontage. The moon, almost full, gave her enough light to see where she was going. She felt suddenly, inexplicably lonely.

She saw some rocks on the beach ahead and made her way toward them, thinking to sit a while. Then she saw movement, and paused, narrowing her eyes. A man was coming from among the rocks, heading in her direction. She gave a tiny gasp of fright, then as he drew closer, her fear vanished, to be replaced by something else that made her heart beat crazily in her chest.

It was Dominic. She stopped walking and stood motionless until he reached her. He looked at her and said nothing for a moment. Finally he touched her arm. "You look like a moon goddess."

Ridiculously pleased by his words,

Jane replied, "Not a Mayan one, I hope," she said, laughing to cover her blush.

"No. The more traditional type. Lovely and glowing."

Jane didn't know what to say to that. Seeming to sense her embarrassment, Dominic took her hand and led her over to the rocky area. "Come on. Let's pull up a rock and sit. I'm getting sick of my own company."

"But the others are here now." Jane wanted to bite off her tongue. She was afraid he'd ask how she knew. How she'd seen them in the dining-room but hadn't joined them.

He spared her. "Yes, but they've all gone to their rooms for the night. We're starting, early tomorrow. Me, I can't go to sleep that early."

They found a wide, flat boulder and sat on it, the sides of their bodies almost touching. They were silent for a time, watching the moon's reflection off the sea, until at last Dom asked, "Where's Dee? I thought I might have

160

seen the pair of you in the dining-room."

"Well, she's a little under the weather." The pun had slipped out. Jane hadn't meant to be flippant.

"What do you mean?"

"She's got a sunburn."

Dominic's head shot up. "A sunburn? How bad?"

Jane was surprised at the intense concern in his voice. Lots of people got sunburns when they went on holiday. Suddenly she understood. Tomato-red complexions probably didn't photo-graph too well. She was relieved that his concern was not personal. And then chastized herself for being relieved.

"I don't think you have to worry, Dominic. The burn's in an area that, well, let's just say it probably won't be needed for your photography. Just don't force her to, um, sit on a cactus."

His brows drew together briefly. "I wouldn't force anybody to sit on a — oh, I take your meaning." He gave a hoot of laughter. "That girl. I told her it might be a good idea to get as much of an all-over tan as she could, but how . . . ?"

"She calls it a bikini, but it's really just a piece of string. She was too embarrassed to be seen putting sunscreen there, and so . . . "

Dominic laughed out loud. "Only Dee. This could only happen to her." He threw a companionable arm across Jane's shoulders, and Jane marvelled at how natural, how right it felt. Gone was her initial unease. She laughed, too, and the sound was whisked away on the breeze.

He turned to her then. "Jane, I'm going to be pretty busy this week, but I hope we can get together again."

"Oh, I'm sure we will," she said lightly, as if the idea were of little consequence. "You'll be around in the evenings, I imagine. I'm sure you and your staff and my niece have lots to talk about. I'll no doubt see you in the dining-room, or around the pool, or — "

"I mean just you and me."

"You do?" Jane said, and her heart raced.

"Why does that surprise you, Jane? I like your company. You're a breath of fresh air to me. You're not like other women — "

"That's just it. I'm not. At least not like the ones you know. You made a point of telling me once — " she hesitated " — I'm not your type. You like tall elegant models, gorgeous women — "

"Did I say you weren't my type? Funny, I don't remember saying that, and if I did, I must have been teasing," he said thoughtfully. "As for models, well, I like to photograph them, not necessarily spend my personal time with them. Why do you keep putting yourself down, Jane? Don't you think you're worth seeing?"

"Of course I am, but not by glamorous photographers. I can only think that I'm just convenient for you somehow."

"No. You're wrong." His voice was low, gentle. The arm around her shoulders tightened. With his free hand he touched her cheek and turned her face toward his. She could feel his warm breath on her skin. He's going to kiss me, Jane thought. It's going to happen now. It mustn't, I said it wouldn't . . . but I want it, I want it . . .

He bent his head, and when his mouth touched hers Jane felt almost faint with excitement. Yet she was also filled with a sense that kissing him was the natural order of things, as natural as sitting on a rock on a tropical beach with him, feeling the breeze, the gentle murmur of the sea.

She leaned into him, parted her lips, and as the kiss grew more urgent, she suddenly pulled away. "No . . . no. We can't. I . . . Deirdre . . . "

He sat up, grasped her shoulders to turn her to face him and said hoarsely, incredulously, "What has Deirdre got to do with anything?"

Jane didn't want to explain to him that her niece was in love with him and saw her aunt as competition. That Deirdre would be terribly hurt.

And that she, herself, might be terribly hurt.

"Well, the shoot and all, you know . . . " she said vaguely.

"God only knows what you're trying to say, or rather not to say, but it *is* getting late." He looked at her in the moonlight, saying nothing for several moments, then shook his head. "Jane, I want to see you this week. Just you. I'll find a way."

He stopped and studied her flushed face closely. "I think you're afraid of me. Don't be."

All very well for him to say, Jane thought later as she lay sleepless in her bed, for she was afraid. Deathly afraid.

8

THE sun dropped out of the sky. The hotel terrace was starting to fill with guests, dressed in outfits designed to show off newly acquired tans and seeking before-dinner cocktails. Jane realized she had better make herself scarce if she didn't want to encounter the group returning from the shoot in Tulum.

That morning, before heading out, Deirdre had dropped by Jane's room to report that her sunburn wasn't as painful and she'd spread it with a soothing cream. She also mentioned that they'd probably be back for dinner. Jane had spent the day relaxing, sunbathing and swimming, thinking to finish the novel she'd begun the night before. Further excursions to Mayan ruins could wait a day or two.

As she inserted a Book Nook

bookmark into place and was about to drop the novel into her bag, she heard a woman's voice call hello.

She looked up and was surprised to see Joss, Dominic's assistant. "Jane," the older woman said, "Join me for a drink?"

Jane hadn't seen Joss since the day she'd been in the studio watching the shoot with Monique. The middle-aged dynamo hadn't been particularly friendly then, though she hadn't been openly hostile. So Jane was surprised now that Joss was actually seeking her company.

"Okay," she said, seeing no graceful way out of this. "That would be nice."

A few minutes later they were sitting sipping their drinks — Jane's a frothy and icy barman's special, which was a fruit shake with a splash of grenadine, and Joss's a 'something harder, please', which was a scotch and soda. Jane, uncomfortable with the silence, asked Joss how the shoot had gone.

"Gruelling," was the answer. "Dominic

167

wasn't satisfied with anything. The light, the angles, the way the clothes hung. Phew. Sometimes he can be such a slave-driver."

"Then why do you work for him?"

"Because he's the best." Joss's face creased into a smile. "I guess I just like to complain. And while we're on the subject of my orneriness, I'd like to apologize to you for my rudeness those first couple of times we met."

"No apology necessary, Joss. I barged in on things, especially that one evening — "

"Say no more. Dominic told me about the hunt for Dee. I have a daughter of my own who I worry about. Your niece reminds me of her a little. Headstrong and boy-crazy — or maybe I should say man-crazy."

Jane lowered her glass. "You've noticed?"

"Only an idiot wouldn't notice. *And* the man in question. Dominic thinks Dee just sort of hero worships him, and isn't that sweet. But I think it's more serious than that, and actually that's one reason I wanted a chance to talk to you about it."

"I'm glad," Jane said honestly. "I need someone to talk to about Deirdre."

Joss nodded. "She seems to be getting worse. You should have seen her today. When she wasn't on camera, she just stood there looking at Dom like a lovesick calf, and when she was on camera, well, the way she reacted to Dom's instructions — you know how he sort of croons . . . "

Yes, thought Jane, thinking of the session in his studio with the lovely Monique, and even the way he'd talked her own reluctant self into actually enjoying getting her picture taken.

" . . . was enough to make me want to scream," Joss went on. "And when the shoot was over, she glued herself to his side and practically pleaded with him to take her out to dinner. Dom seemed quite oblivious to the fact that she meant just her, and he invited everyone to some restaurant in Cancun, Dee had murder in her eye."

Jane grimaced, and Joss continued, her tone less harsh, "Dominic Slater is quite a guy, so I can understand your niece's crush. And he has, of course, dated models, but he doesn't seem to much any more, though. I suppose his marriage to Katya soured him on that."

"Really?" Jane said. "I saw him at a play a couple of weeks ago with . . . Karen, I think her name was."

"Ah, Karen. Well, that's neither here nor there. She probably asked him out. Or rather, insisted he take her. He's a marshmallow at heart. Tough professionally, but personally that's another story. Doesn't know how to say no."

Jane recalled the way he had pulled Karen possessively to his side — was that being a marshmallow? — but she also recalled his kind treatment of the young purse snatcher. "What was his wife like?" she asked. "If you want to tell me it's none of my business, I'll understand."

"Nonsense. I've no qualms about talking about that woman. I hate her."

Jane looked at Joss in surprise. "Really? Why?"

"Because of what she did to Dom. He doesn't deserve to be treated that way. God, it was classic. He marries her because she's the most beautiful woman he's ever seen. He assumes she's just as beautiful on the inside as on the outside. 'Katya,' I remember him saying to me once, just before they were married, 'even her name is like a poem'." Joss sighed and shook her head. "Besotted fool. I told him as much, but of course he wasn't about to listen to me. He was young and headstrong and — well, at least now he's older and wiser. Also cynical. Katya did that to him in a hurry. He went in to that marriage with all his romantic idealism intact. He came out with it, and himself, in little pieces."

Jane listened to the story in

astonishment. "I thought they were madly in love."

"That's what Dom thought, too, for a while. But it turned out he was the only one feeling that way. He came home a day early from a shoot on location in the Bahamas, and found her with another man. In his own home, furthermore." Joss shook her head. "He was devastated."

So they did have something else in common, Jane thought. Betrayal. Not much of a footing for a relationship. "I don't understand people like that," she said aloud. "People who use someone else's love. Take it, and then abuse it."

Joss looked at her kindly. "No, I can see you're the sort of person who wouldn't do that. Forgive me for sounding like a meddling old woman, but I can't help but think you and Dom — "

"No!" Jane nearly shouted. "No," she repeated more softly, "we're not at all suited to each other. I'm not his type."

"Don't be so sure, Jane," was all Joss said. "Don't be so sure."

★ ★ ★

On Tuesday morning Jane visited the ruins at Coba. She'd found Miguel, the English-speaking Mayan driver who had brought her and Deirdre from the airport, on the hotel drive-through, and she leapt into his cab gratefully. With his knowledge of English and local history, he'd be perfect.

He was a great guide, but the day was hot, arduous and exhausting. Back in the hotel a few hours later, Jane changed quickly into her suit and coverup, grabbed her novel and a towel and headed for the elevator. As she rode down she thought about Deirdre. And she thought about Dom. She hadn't seen the group returning from dinner in Cancun the evening before, but she'd heard them through the open door to her balcony. And the voice she'd heard most clearly was her niece's. It trilled and chirped and was sprinkled liberally with "Oh Dom," which elicited a few deep murmured responses. She'd imagined Deirdre was trying to finagle some time alone with Dom, but when Jane had finally given in to her curiosity and gone to peer over her balcony railing, she'd seen Dominic moving off alone toward the cabana area and Deirdre trudging up to the main door.

Jane still hadn't told her niece about the time she'd spent with Dom on Sunday, but now there seemed little point. *I hope we can see each other again*, he'd said. Now, with the passage of a couple of days when he'd made no attempt to see her, she recognized his words for what they were: just spur-of-the-moment things, and quite, quite meaningless.

As the elevator doors slid open, she headed across the lobby and out toward the pool area, hoping it wouldn't be too crowded. At the entrance a quick glance revealed a couple of empty loungers. She headed toward one.

"Jane! Over here!"

Reclining on a lounger on the other side of the pool was Dom, surrounded by his whole entourage, including Deirdre, who sat up looking less than delighted. Dominic patted an empty lounger beside him "Sit. Relax," he said.

Deirdre was clearly put out, because she leapt up and announced it was time for a swim. Sashaying over to the pool's edge, she executed a perfect dive.

Jane sighed, removed her coverup, then stretched out on the lounger and closed her eyes. After a moment, she became aware that she was being observed. The sensation was at once pleasing and unnerving. She knew her stomach was flat, her thighs firm and smooth, her full breasts staying modestly within the confines of her bathing suit. Yet at the same time she feared, particularly in this company that she would be seen to have major flaws. She might be seen as fat — at least in comparison to a model.

Self-consciousness overcome her at last and she opened her eyes. Sure enough Dominic was staring at her.

"Do I pass?" she whispered, not wanting the others to overhear, then allowed her gaze to travel the length of him.

"Do I?" he whispered in return.

"I hate people who answer a question with a question," she said, her mouth quirking drolly.

He inclined his head. "If the question, like yours, is silly, it doesn't require an answer."

Their little conversation had attracted the attention of Joss, however, who said bluntly from her chair a few feet away, "What are you two on about? Either talk loud enough so I can hear you, or be quiet. You make me feel like I should leave the room, or in this case, jump in the pool."

Dominic laughed. "You really are an old busybody, aren't you? But if you really must know, I was just telling

Jane how gorgeous she looks."

"You were?" If Jane had had feathers she would have preened them. Good Lord, she thought, was she so starved for male admiration? How could she be? Hadn't she spent the past few years doing her best to avoid it?

"Hey," Dom said, "how about a swim? You look like you could use one."

Jane did indeed want a swim, but she wished she was alone. For her aquatic skills were rather weak, to say the least, and she felt shy about putting them on display. Especially after the elegant performance of her niece, who dove and swam like an otter.

Dom seemed to guess the cause of her hesitation. "Come on. We won't try to match Esther Williams there — " with a grin he gestured at Deirdre, who was performing a graceful crawl back and forth the length of the pool " — we'll just get in and splash around, okay?"

Jane grinned back. "Okay."

The next couple of hours were spent in and around the pool. Jane couldn't help but notice that Dom, unlike her, was a strong swimmer, but he made her inadequacies seem quite unimportant. When at last everyone had had enough and were collecting their things to return to their rooms to shower and change, Dom invited Jane to join them for dinner. "We're meeting at the dining-room entrance at eight," he said.

Jane promised to be there.

As she rode the elevator up with Deirdre, she sensed all was not well with the girl. Her suspicions were confirmed when Deirdre blurted, "Are you really going to have dinner with us, Jane?" It was clear she hoped Jane would say no.

In fact, Jane did not really feel up to it. Talk would be of the shoot and how it was going, perhaps of the fashion industry in general, in all of which Deirdre played an integral part and Jane did not. "Maybe not," she said.

"I'll see how I feel after a nap and a shower."

As it turned out, Jane's nap was a deep sleep. She awoke to the insistent ringing of her phone. A glance at the bedside clock told her it was ten o'clock.

Only half-awake, she answered, "Hello?"

"Jane. Where were you? We missed you."

It was Dominic. "I . . . I fell asleep, I guess. I didn't mean to. I just — "

"Never mind the excuses. I have the perfect punishment."

Jane snapped fully awake. "What?"

"To pay for your lapse, you must come with me tomorrow morning to see the sunrise in Tulum. You said you wanted to."

She listened in astonishment. He'd remembered. And obviously he'd meant it when he'd said that he wanted to spend some time with her — just the two of them. Her resolution to avoid him was quickly losing ground. "Uh, yes," she said slowly.

"I'll meet you in the lobby at four."

"Four . . . ?"

"Yup, a.m. Sunrise comes early here. We need to get to Tulum by five if we want to bear witness to the event." He hesitated, then, "Still on?"

"Yes." Punishment duly accepted.

★ ★ ★

When her alarm went off at 3.30 Jane awoke in confusion. What was this insistent ringing in the middle of the night? Then she remembered. Sunrise in Tulum. With Dom.

She leapt out of bed, dashed into the shower, and dressed in a pair of light cotton shorts and matching top, all inside of twenty minutes. She stopped to frown at her reflection in the mirror. "Hair from hell," she muttered, as she took a moment to try to impose some order to it. Then she grabbed an oversize sweatshirt on her way out the door, yanking it over her head as she headed to the elevator.

When Dom strode in to the lobby, his glance landed almost instantly on her. He was dressed in faded jeans and pale blue T-shirt, his face tanned from his hours in the sun, his black straight hair slick and shiny from a shower. Jane thought she'd never seen a more beautiful sight.

"Sleep well?" he asked, once they were on their way along the darkened roadway in a rented car.

"Yes," she murmured.

"Me, too." He seemed in a mood to talk, and he added, "This is great. I really wanted an advance preview to see what the light is like there at dawn. Nice not to go alone."

"Glad I could be of service," said Jane.

He heard the dry tone of her voice and, keeping his left hand firmly on the wheel, reached his right over to place it lightly over her mouth. "Shush. Are you always so grumpy in the morning? Obviously you don't realize how good this offer really is."

Jane slapped at his hand playfully. "Oh yeah? Tell me."

Dom sighed. "Lord, but you're a difficult woman. Don't you know anything?" He glanced at her briefly out of the corner of his eye and said, "People should never watch sunsets or sunrises on their own. It's an unwritten law. If you do, you're condemned to a life of loneliness."

"Oh, come on. Where'd you hear that?"

"My maiden aunt Bethesda told me that a long time ago. She said it's what happened to her. She said she was a lonely old woman because when she was young she used to watch sunsets and sunrises by herself." He paused and added, "She *was* a lonely old woman." Then he grinned and kept his gaze fixed on the road ahead. "But then again, it may have been because she was stupid and mean and ugly."

"Oh! You are a rotten human being!" Jane smacked his shoulder.

Dominic trapped her hand with one of his and held it tight against his arm. "Thank you. I need people like you to remind me I'm not perfect."

Jane could only think about how good his touch felt.

When they arrived at Tulum, its ruined structures ghostly in the fading starlight, Dom pulled a flashlight from the glove compartment and they made their way to the same place they had perched Sunday afternoon. Neither felt the need to speak and so they stared out at the dark sea in silence as the faintest of greys began to rise on the horizon. Then slowly, ever so slowly, the sky took on a yellowish hue and distinct golden tentacles jutted from the back of the sea. Still she and Dom were quiet, as if words might break the magic. But as the sun itself crested the horizon, Jane breathed out an audible sigh of awe. Dom's hand moved to rest warmly on her leg just above her knee, and when she responded by leaning her head against his shoulder, he twisted slightly and dropped a sweet, light kiss on her hair.

When the sun had fully risen she turned to him and said simply, "Thank you."

"No. It's I who should thank you, Jane. Now I'll never be lonely again. Nor will you."

Jane looked at him wonderingly. "Tell me. Tell me about . . . Katya." Even though Joss had told her a good deal, she wanted to hear it from him.

He didn't object. His gaze fixed on the horizon, he began to speak, slowly, hesitantly, as if every word were painful. "I once felt that my wife was perfect for me. That she embodied everything that's beautiful in a woman. When we split up, I threw myself into my work as an escape from loneliness. It took me a while to understand that I'd been in love with someone who didn't exist. I wasn't really seeing her. I was seeing only what she wanted me to see. She was exquisitely lovely, and it was all on the outside." He added bitterly, "But I learned something from the experience."

"What?"

"That the condition of 'being in love' isn't real. That it's easy to fall in love with what you think someone is — not what they really are. I fell in love with a woman I thought was ideal. She was anything but." Abruptly he turned his head and fixed his gaze on Jane. "You know what I'm talking about, don't you? I can see it in your eyes."

She was about to blurt out that she'd had a similar experience, but something — the feeling that he wasn't being completely honest? — stopped her. For she recalled the photo of Katya on his living-room wall, wondered why he kept it there if he disliked her.

Dom was the one to break the prolonged silence. "Jane," he said, twisting away a little, his hand breaking contact with her leg. Jane was amazed at how bereft she felt. His voice was soft. "Do you remember when I was taking photographs of you? And I asked you to think of someone?"

"Yes," she said cautiously.

"Well, *is* there someone?"

She thought of Fred. Dear, sweet, safe Fred. "No," she said softly, "not really."

"Good." After a few more minutes had passed without a word spoken by either of them, he said, "We'd better head back. The others are expecting me at breakfast, and then we're off to Coba to do some shots there."

They began walking to the car. Suddenly he stopped and looked at her. "I know you've already visited Coba . . . but would you like to go there again? Watch the shoot?"

"I . . . I don't know. Wouldn't I just be in the way? And maybe people, er, Deirdre, won't appreciate my being there."

"What, my little moon goddess, are you talking about? Why on earth should Dee mind your being there?"

Jane couldn't ignore the foolish thrill his calling her 'my little moon goddess' had sent through her. Every time she thought his words were meaningless, delivered in a light-hearted fashion for her momentary amusement, he startled her by showing that he remembered the little things. Such as what he'd said while photographing her; such as telling her she looked like a moon goddess later that same day.

"Oh, I just thought maybe having her aunt there might inhibit Dee somehow, and — "

He barked out a laugh. "Dee? Inhibited? Are we talking about the girl who puts on a piece of string and three Bandaids, calls it a bathing suit, and prances about at the hotel pool?"

"Well, yes, there is that," Jane said with an answering laugh. Then, "I'd love to go."

He met her eyes and said simply, "Good. I'm glad."

9

"THAT'S it, Dee! keep moving like that . . . look this way . . . shoulders forward . . . head back . . . beautiful . . . perfect . . . Yes, yes, so lovely . . . "

Jane watched her niece's languid, graceful movements and could see why she was so in demand as a model. Deirdre was positioned on a step several feet above the base of one of Coba's ancient pyramids, a tanned leg escaping from the soft folds of the silky coverup she wore, her lovely neck arched.

"Let's take a break," Dominic called. "We've been at it for an hour, and in this heat, an hour's like a day." He walked closer to Deirdre and looked up at her. "Come down off that pyramid, my love. Before you melt and we have to wipe you off." He grinned and held out his hand.

Deirdre bestowed her most bewitching smile on Dom, then took a couple of steps and reached for his hand. As she moved, she stumbled and fell against his chest. She flung her arms around him, gasping.

Had she really lost her footing and nearly fallen? Jane wondered. As she stood there meanly doubting her niece's action, Dom gently unwound Dee's arms from around his neck, laughing as he did so. "How is it you're so graceful when I'm taking your picture, then you turn into an ox when we're through, Dee?"

Deirdre's only response was to trill delightedly back at him and link one slim tanned arm with his.

"See what I mean?" came Joss's hushed voice from behind Jane.

Jane sighed. "Yes, but we're only here for a couple more days, and Deirdre goes home to Iowa at the end of the summer, so . . . "

"I don't know if anyone's told you, Jane," said Joss, still *sotto voce*, "but

Dom is doing another shoot in Puerto Vallarta next week, and he wants — "

"Joss! Over here."

Joss threw Jane a beleaguered glance. "My master calls. I'll catch up with you later."

Jane remained at the shoot only long enough to down another soft drink and have a brief chat with Dom and the ever-clinging Deirdre. She listened as Deirdre launched into her usual praise. "Isn't Dom divine? And did you see the things he can make me do?"

She took note of the almost paternal pride in Dom's voice as he replied, "Dee, it's you. You're a fantastic model."

Enough of this, thought Jane, and pleading heat exhaustion, she trekked back to the parking lot and collapsed into a waiting cab.

★ ★ ★

Jane spent the rest of the afternoon reading a book about the decline and fall of the Mayan civilization, which she'd bought in the hotel shop, and writing a letter to Sharon. She reassured her sister as best she could that all was well, even though that wasn't entirely true. Late in the afternoon she found Miguel outside the hotel and had him drive her into Cancun. She did a little shopping — a pair of silver earrings for Nancy, a leather wallet for Fred — and then enjoyed a Mexican meal of spicy *riz con pollo* at a café.

By the time she got back to the Hotel d'Oro, it was almost eight o'clock and Dominic and Deirdre and company had still not returned. Probably they had stopped off somewhere for dinner. That was fine with Jane. She still hadn't been able to get any real fix on what was happening between Dom and her, nor was she even sure anything actually was. She decided as she got ready for bed that the morning's early interlude in Tulum was just that. An interlude. Extremely pleasant, but foolish to imagine it was anything more.

She had just dropped off when there was a knock at her door. "Yes?" she called out, hoping against foolish hope it was Dominic.

Deirdre answered her. "Jane, it's me. You're not asleep, are you?"

"Not now," Jane said.

She got up and padded to the door. "Come on in, sweetie." She took in her niece's unusually dishevelled appearance. "What's up?"

"We got caught in the rain."

"It's raining?"

"Yeah. Like crazy! I came back with Dom and Joss in his car. We stopped at a restaurant on the way, and by the time we got back here we had to run from the car to the hotel because it was pouring."

Jane made sympathetic noises, but felt her stomach tighten. Why was Deirdre, despite her dripping hair and wet clothing, looking as if she'd just scored a winning touchdown? She had a feeling she was about to find out.

"Dom's doing a shoot in Puerto

Vallarta next week," Deirdre began, barely able to contain her excitement, "and he says he wants me to come! He says I'm perfect. Just the look the client wants! Isn't that great?"

Jane sat down on the edge of her bed and closed her eyes. So that was what Joss had started to tell her earlier. And why hadn't Dom mentioned this to her when they were in Tulum? He must have known about it then, and how impossible it was for Dee to go. It was cruel to get the girl all keyed up over something that would have to be snatched away. Damn him, she thought.

"Deirdre," she said, raising her eyes to her exuberant niece, "it's great . . . and it's not great. You know there's no way you can go."

Deirdre looked like a child who'd just been told there is no Father Christmas. "What do you mean? Why not?"

"You know why not. I can't take another week off work and there's no way your mother's going to let you go without me. It's as simple as that. I'm sorry."

"You . . . you're not sorry, Jane! You're not sorry at all!" Deirdre cried, her voice and eyes ablaze with accusation. "You just don't want me to go because of Dom. I've seen the way you act around him! You want him for yourself, and you can't stand the thought of him going anywhere with me. You — "

"Stop it!" Jane commanded. "You don't know what you're saying. I am *not* concerned about Dom. It's you and this crazy crush you have on him. Dammit, Deirdre, open your eyes. He's a sophisticated older man. He's fond of you. He thinks you're a wonderful model. His asking you to go to Puerto Vallarta has nothing to do with personal feelings. He just thinks you'd be great for the job. Why can't you see that?"

But Jane's last words were spoken to the slammed hotel-room door. She slumped her shoulders in defeat. Instead of this time in Cancun showing

Deirdre that Dominic was way out of her league, the girl was convinced more than ever that Dominic was the man for her. His asking her to come on a shoot the following week made the situation even worse. And Jane's having to play the 'heavy' made her furious. She was tired of her niece seeing her as some sort of ogre. She had a sudden urge to go seek out Dominic now, ask him why he hadn't discussed this with her first. But then her rational side asserted itself. Best to wait till tomorrow when she felt calmer. When she'd had time to think about what she would say to him.

Jane got up and went to the window. She opened the curtain and peered out. It was indeed raining, hard.

★ ★ ★

The mid-afternoon sun was blinding. And hot. As she looked out over the shimmering sea, Jane stowed away her regrets at having slept late that morning. She had unfortunately missed catching Dom before he went off for the day, and so she'd have to make a point of talking to him later.

She had decided after lunch that a swim was in order. Maybe a little exercise would improve her mood. She'd donned her suit, grabbed a towel and headed down to the beach. She would have preferred the pool, but she didn't want to risk encountering anyone from the shoot. They might have called quits early, as they had the other day. She wanted to see Dom, true, but *alone*.

At the beach she'd waded through ankle-deep water to its far end, near the spot where she and Dominic had been Sunday night. She was the only person for a hundred yards, and that suited her mood perfectly.

Leaving her towel and book on the sand, she ran into the sea. The water was warm, yet still refreshing. She floated on her back for a while and tried to relax, empty her mind. But Dominic kept intruding. Her desire to see him again was almost overwhelming. And not just to talk about this business of Deirdre's going to Puerto Vallarta. Despite all her resolutions to the contrary and her belief that Dom was no danger to her, the memory of the closeness they'd shared the day before filled her with longing. She wanted almost desperately to recapture it.

A wave splashed over Jane's face. Startled, she breathed in sharply, and her reward was a mouthful of salty water. She spluttered, then turned her head and saw how far she'd drifted from shore. She rolled on to her stomach, faced the shore and began doing her version of the breaststroke. Yet with every sweep of her arms, every kick of her legs, the beach seemed no closer. And was it her imagination, or was the water less friendly now, the waves rougher, splashing into her face, the salt stinging her eyes, clogging her nose? When she imagined she felt something brush her legs, she screamed, gulped more water and went under. She fought her way back to the choppy surface, gasped for air and was again rewarded with a mouthful of water. She choked, and panic overtook her completely. Her arms flailed, her shouts for help came in short bursts. The last thing she was aware of was the sound of someone shouting, far away, before she sank beneath the waves and knew only darkness.

* * *

Jane was reluctant to let go of her dream. She was being cradled in warm, strong arms. Dom's face was in front of her, and he was kissing her softly. It felt so good, so right, so wonderful. Then his deep, voice was murmuring, "Jane. Jane. My little Jane . . . "

Jane's eyes fluttered open, and she realized her dream and reality were one. She was lying in a bed with cool fresh sheets, and Dom was leaning over her and looking into her eyes and smiling warmly.

"Ah, so you're awake at last," he said. "For a moment there I thought you were going to sleep till Christmas."

"I . . . " Jane began, then stopped, confused. "Where am I?"

Dom sat back and looked at her. "My cabana. Don't you remember?"

"No. I mean, I was swimming and . . . "

" . . . and having trouble." He paused and shook his head. "Fortunately our shoot ended early. I went looking for you the minute we got back, and when I found out you weren't in your room or around the pool, I went down to the beach and saw you out there. Don't you remember me shouting your name?"

Jane closed her eyes for a moment. "Yes. Yes, I remember now, but then what happened? How'd I get to shore?" She paused and looked at him questioningly. "You . . . ?"

"Yes, I hauled you in." His expression changed, and he said, "Don't think about it. You're safe now. I just thank

God I was there . . . " His voice cracked a little.

Despite the warmth of the covers, Jane suddenly began to shiver, and her eyes filled with tears. Dominic pulled her quivering body up and held her to him, one hand making soothing circles on her back. A delicious warmth spread through her. His voice was murmuring, "I thought I'd lost you, Jane. I was so scared. So scared . . . "

Jane rubbed a fist in the corner of one eye, wiping away the moisture. "I owe you my life, Dom. I never would have made it out of that water on my own. She tilted her face up and kissed him tentatively, the touch a mix of gratitude, and something far stronger. With a groan Dom responded, pulling her unresisting body closer and deepening the kiss. Jane found herself responding completely, uncaring of where it could lead, considering the fact she was in his bed — "

Suddenly he pressed himself away from her, then tucked her tousled head into the hollow of his neck and shoulder. "You're in no condition for this," he murmured.

For kissing? Jane wanted to protest. But of course he had meant more than kissing, and she realized she probably wouldn't have had the strength to stop him.

"I have no right to take advantage of you when you're . . . like this. It's too easy for me to get carried away with you. You're so vulnerable, so sweet, so very beautiful . . . "

Jane didn't believe that at all. Beautiful? How could she be beautiful, especially now, with her hair an impossible tangle, her eyes puffy with tears, her clothing — ?

It was then that Jane noticed she was wearing one of his shirts. A glance over his shoulder revealed her swimsuit hanging from the arm of the cane chair, her towel in a heap beside it. She found she did not feel at all embarrassed at the thought of how that had come about. She was, though, embarrassed by his compliment.

"Hm, well, uh, I know I'm not those things, but thank you for saying so . . . "

She'd kept her face hidden at his neck and shoulder as she spoke, but he set his hands on her shoulders and pushed her away slightly.

"Raise your eyes," he commanded gently but firmly. "Look at me."

Reluctantly Jane did as he said until her green gaze met the all-seeing blue of his.

"Jane, it's okay," he said. "When are you going to learn to accept the fact that you're a beautiful and desirable woman?" He paused. "Who did this to you? What man made you think you weren't good enough?"

Jane was astonished by his perception. And even more astonished that her past should concern him. "I . . . I was just young and foolish," she murmured. "And I thought he loved me. He seemed so perfect — " Jane stopped abruptly, suddenly aware that she had echoed Dom's own words about Katya.

"You thought he was something he wasn't, didn't you? It's an easy mistake to make," Dom said gently. "I know one thing — you weren't a fool. He was."

He pulled her close and hugged her again. "And now," he said quietly, "I have something I must tell you."

"What?" Her voice was tremulous.

"I'm starving!"

Jane wasn't sure what she'd expected him to say, but then her stomach rumbled. "Yes, me too," she said, smiling.

Dom laughed and got to his feet. As he strode over to the small table by the window and picked up the tray that sat there, he said, "A real gourmet treat. I picked it up while you were sleeping. A pot of tea, and the pièce de résistance — " he paused for effect — "cheese sandwiches!"

"Ooh la-la!" Jane exclaimed, laughing and finding relief at the silliness. "But how did you find plain old cheese sandwiches in Mexico?"

"Trust me, it wasn't easy," he said, as he put the tray down on the bed and began unwrapping one of the sandwiches. "But I thought burritos and stuffed chilli peppers were not perhaps the best thing for you right now."

Jane looked at him adoringly.

★ ★ ★

"Where's Deirdre, anyway?" Jane asked, leaning back against the headboard of the bed. She felt considerably better now, after the tea and sandwiches. "I'd better get going back to my room. She'll be worried . . ."

"No, she's fine. She and Joss and the others are busy eating in the dining-room even as we speak. They were privy to the tail end of my rescue operation he stopped to grin at Jane and reach out a finger to stroke her cheek " — and Dee knows you're here. She certainly didn't seem very

204

happy about the idea of my bringing you to my cabana, but I assured her I'd take good care of you and let her know when you came to. I'll do that when I take you back to your room."

Jane could well imagine that Deirdre would not have been too happy about Don's bringing her to his cabana, but for quite a different reason than Dom had assumed. "Jane," Dom said next, putting his hands on her shoulders, "I want us to spend some time together tomorrow. Do you?"

"But how?" Jane asked, thrilled that he wanted to see her. "Aren't you working?"

"Just in the morning, Jane. We'll be through by noon. The others were talking about going to Cozumel for the afternoon and doing some snorkelling. But I don't imagine that, after this afternoon's adventure, you'd be too keen on that, so — " he paused briefly to flick a breadcrumb from the corner of her mouth " — I thought you and I could take the ferry to the Isla Mujeres.

It's a lovely little island, and not nearly as long a trip as Cozumel is. Besides, I'd like to get away from the others and just be with you." His eyebrows lifted questioningly, disarmingly.

Jane nodded, then remembered her earlier plan — Lord, was it only that morning? — to upbraid Dom about his asking Deirdre if she could go to Puerto Vallarta the next week. She'd been so angry! Where had all that anger gone?

"I meant to talk to you about next week, Dom," she said in reasonable tones. "I almost forgot . . . "

"Ah, yes," he said. "Puerto Vallarta. In today's excitement — " he smiled and touched her cheek " — I almost forgot, too."

"Why," Jane asked, trying her best to sound like a concerned parent, "didn't you tell me you wanted Deirdre to go on that shoot?"

"I meant to," he replied, a note of genuine regret in his voice. "But I'd only found out when we were in Coba that the model scheduled for the shoot wouldn't be arriving till mid-week, and I suddenly had this great idea that we could use Dee for the first couple of days. I'd actually hoped maybe you could find a way to come along. Puerto Vallarta is on the Pacific." He paused. "And the sunsets are great."

He'd hoped she could go along? Jane closed her eyes and imagined watching a sunset with Dom. "I can't," she said woefully. "I've got to get back to New York and the shop."

"Well," he said on a heavy sigh, "you wouldn't have to worry about Dee. She'd be in safe hands. Especially if I ask Joss to keep an eye on her when I can't. Besides, it'd be only for three days. You're going home on Saturday, right? She could fly home late Tuesday afternoon . . . "

Jane was torn. Now was the time to tell him how Deirdre felt about him. Why it had become a problem.

"Well, I — "

"Please say yes, Jane. You'll really be

helping me out of a bind. The model scheduled — "

"Who is the model scheduled, anyway?" Jane interjected.

Dominic frowned and looked away. Jane felt a sudden prick of fear. After a moment, he said, "Someone I really don't care to work with." A pause. "Katya. My ex-wife."

Jane sucked in a deep breath, then closed her eyes, hoping to calm the quick sick flutter in her stomach. "Oh," was all she could manage to respond.

"The main reason I'd like Dee for the shoot is that she and Katya bear a striking resemblance to each other. Dee is far more pleasant to work with, and frankly, I think she's a better model for the job — younger and possessing the truly fresh look the client wants. So if I use both of them, show the pictures to the client, I think he'll prefer Dee. It could mean a lot of extra exposure for her. More money, too, to pay for that college education you say her parents want her to have."

Jane tried desperately to collect her thoughts. To let her common sense override the emotional jolt she'd felt at the idea of him working with the woman he *said* he no longer cared for.

At last, though, she resolved to say nothing more about Katya. It really wasn't any of her business, anyway, whether Dom still, to use Deirdre's words, carried a torch for the lovely model, consciously or unconsciously. "Okay. I think I can persuade her mother. And since it's only for a couple of days . . . "

Dom grabbed her and gave her a big hug. "Baby," he said, laughing, "as Ralph Cramden says, you're the greatest!"

Jane laughed and hugged him back. "I just hope I'm not the greatest fool!"

10

THE next morning, Jane awoke with the pleasurable anticipation of the coming excursion to Isla Mujeres — but also despairing of the nasty scene with Deirdre just before going to bed.

Dom had been walking her back to the main building of the hotel the evening before and they'd run into Deirdre in the lobby. The girl had rushed up to them, screaming breathlessly, "Oh, Jane! You're okay now. Thank heaven!"

Then she'd instantly turned her attention to Dom. She'd thrown her arms around him and kissed him squarely on his startled mouth. "Thank you, thank you! You saved Aunt Jane's life. You're a hero! I think you're wonderful!"

Jane noticed the stress on the word

'aunt' and how Deirdre seemed to forget about her for a moment, and when the girl did at last peel her young, tanned body from Dom's, she'd grasped Jane's arm firmly and said, "Come on, Aunt Jane. I'll take you to your room. Dom's done enough. It's time he got a break."

Dom's eyebrows had risen at that, but it seemed he had no choice. Deirdre, despite her youth, could be quite a force when she chose. And this was definitely one of those moments. Fortunately, while still back in his cabana, he and Jane had already established their plans for the next day — this after a long and warm kiss good-night.

So Deirdre had accompanied Jane up in the elevator, chattering about Dom's 'fabulous' rescue the whole time. She followed Jane down the hallway and into Jane's room, her mouth still working at a furious pace.

"Boy," she said. "I wish it had been me, not you. You're so lucky!"

"Lucky? I nearly drowned. I don't call that lucky . . . "

"I mean, getting rescued by Dom. And then — " Deirdre's eyes narrowed " — having him take you to his cabana to recover."

"Oh, well, um . . . yes," Jane said stumblingly.

Deirdre went on breezily, "Dom and I had such a great shoot today. He said that he was going to speak to you about my going to Puerto Vallarta. He said that he really wants me to go." She threw her aunt an I-told-you-so glance.

Jane bit back the urge to lecture her niece yet again about Dom's motivation. Instead she said simply, "Dom and I talked about it, and I called your mother, and yes, you can go — "

Deirdre jumped in the air and clapped her hands.

" — but you'll be flying back to New York on Tuesday, so it's just for a couple of days, okay?"

"Three days," Deirdre corrected her triumphantly. She hugged herself and did a little pirouette around the room. When she stopped whirling, she turned to Jane and said, "Guess what? We're all going to Cozumel to do some snorkelling tomorrow. I'm gonna get him to show me how!"

Now was the moment. "Deirdre, Dom is taking me to Isla Mujeres tomorrow."

Jane's statement was met with shocked silence. Then Deirdre spun around and confronted her aunt. "No! He's coming with us!"

Oh Lord, Jane had thought, help me through this.

"Deirdre," she said, her tone conciliatory, almost apologetic, "Dom has offered to take me for a relaxing afternoon on our own — you know how I hate being in a group. I think it's to make up for today's trauma — he's taking pity on me." Jane laughed lightly, hoping to make Deirdre see the unimportance of Dom's gesture. "Besides, he's spent all week with you guys and he'll be spending the next few days with you, and maybe he just wants a change of company. It's just a simple excursion."

Deirdre had reeled on her furiously. "You know how I feel about him! How could you do this to me? This is just like the day back on New York when you went to that shoot, and then had lunch with him! You were trying to steal him away from me then, and you're trying to do it now." Tears sprang to her lovely eyes. "I hate you!" she screeched. "I . . . wish you'd drowned!"

In the bright light of morning, the recollection was no less painful. But at least when Jane saw Dom today, it would be with Deirdre's knowledge. She wouldn't have to hide it from her niece. It was almost a relief. Besides, what she'd said to Deirdre about her outing with Dom today being just a simple excursion was true.

After this week, life would go back to

normal. She'd be home in New York, Dom would be in Puerto Vallarta for another week, and when he was back in New York, he would have forgotten all about her.

Jane flopped back against the pillows as the realization swept over her. He might forget her, but she had fallen in love with him.

She sighed in dismay. This was exactly what she'd spent years trying to avoid. But she would get over him eventually. After all, she'd only known him a short time.

★ ★ ★

It was noon. Dom said he'd come to her room to get her at 12.30. After collecting her book, lotion and towel, she headed out of the pool area and into the hotel lobby. As she rode to her floor, her excitement seemed to rise right along with the elevator. In her room she quickly changed into a pair of soft pink, cotton walking shorts and a matching tank top, then jammed a dry swimsuit and fresh towel into a bag. Her timing was perfect. No sooner had she pulled her hair back with some tortoiseshell combs and poked her feet into a pair of comfortable white sandals, when there was a knock on her door.

"You look good enough to eat," Dom said as he stood surveying her from the doorway. "Pink becomes you, especially with your tan."

Jane blushed the colour of her outfit. Dom stepped further into the room and grabbed her hand. "Let's get moving. There's a ferry in twenty minutes. Oh, wait, one thing . . . "

Dom stopped, dropped her hand and put both of his on either side of her face. Then he placed a warm kiss on her slightly parted lips.

"There," he said when he pulled away. "I've been waiting to do that all day." Grinning, he grabbed her hand again. "We're off to the island of women. Think they'll take a man?"

Jane laughed delightedly.

The ferry, if indeed the small, flat, open boat could be called that, to Isla Mujeres was almost full. Jane and Dom managed to get a spot to stand at the rail, and they watched the island on the horizon as the boat trudged toward it. The trip was only twenty minutes, but Jane thought it was one of the most entertaining twenty minutes she'd ever spent, with Dom and her trading information on the history of Isla Mujeres.

"It's called that because — " he'd begun, only to have Jane interrupt like an enthusiastic schoolgirl.

"I know why, I know why," she said. "The early Spanish Conquistadors called it the Island of Women because the Mayas they encountered there had all sorts of female idols representing Ixchel, the goddess of fertility."

"Well," Dom said, "I see you've been doing your homework. But I think it was more likely named by the pirates of the seventeenth century. They were in the habit of leaving their women there while they went off raiding and pillaging all over the Caribbean."

"Hmph," scoffed Jane. "I think my version is far more pleasant than yours."

Dom snorted and shook his head. "How like a woman!"

"If you," said Jane, laughing, "have such contempt for women, then why are we going to Isla Mujeres, huh? Tell me that!"

Dom threw his arm around Jane's shoulders and pulled her close. "You, my little moon goddess, know perfectly well I don't have contempt for women. I have nothing but the greatest respect for them — even if they do sometimes behave in strange and mysterious ways."

Jane's body was tingling with the contact. "I guess female ways might seem that way to anyone from an alien planet."

Dom pinched her arm and Jane squealed. "Ouch! What was that for?"

"My woman has such a smart mouth. I don't know if I can handle it."

My woman. Jane felt such a surge of pleasure she wasn't sure she could conceal it. His woman. Did he really think of her that way?

★ ★ ★

When they docked at the small town on the northern tip of the island, the first thing they did was rent mopeds. "It's a great way to get around," said Dom.

"This is gorgeous," breathed Jane as she looked at the gleaming white sand of the deserted leeward beach they found. She turned her gaze out to a sea that was much calmer than that in Cancun.

"Yes, isn't it?" agreed Dom. "I thought perhaps you wouldn't mind swimming here."

"Oh," Jane replied, "I don't know about that. I . . . I'm not sure I ever want to swim in the ocean again."

"Nonsense," said Dom firmly. "There's no undertow here, and I think you'd enjoy it." He smiled reassuringly at her. "Come on, Jane," he said as they stretched their towels side by side on the sand. "You know the story about how important it is to get back on a horse after you fall off?"

"You think I should go in the water after my experience yesterday?" Jane was decidedly doubtful. "A pool, yes, but the ocean?"

"Definitely," Dom said. "Besides, I won't let you out of my sight for a moment."

He reached out, took one of her hands in his and squeezed it. Jane didn't think she'd ever felt so safe, protected . . . cared for.

Dom kept his promise as they swam, splashed and played in the water. The beach was the kind that was shallow for a good distance out, and Jane was pretty sure she never once was in over her head. And even if she had been, Dom was right at her side.

After their swim, they ran up the sand hand in hand and threw themselves down on their towels. Jane reached into her bag and pulled out a papaya and a small knife. "Want some?" she offered, cutting off a small piece and extending it toward Dom.

In answer, he leaned closer and opened his mouth. Jane obligingly placed the juicy morsel on his tongue.

"More," he said, when he'd finished the piece. "More."

Laughing, Jane said, "Why, you greedy thing you." Her eyes gleamed. "If you want more, I'm afraid you're going to have to come get it!"

And with that, Jane leapt to her feet, papaya in hand, and began to race down the beach. Dom jumped up and took after her, and it wasn't long before he caught up to her, grasping her by the arm and spinning her around to face him.

"For that," he growled, "you must pay."

And he pulled her hard against his

chest and kissed her, soundly.

At last, breathless and panting, they pulled apart, and still touching — Jane with her hands at his waist, his hands at the nape of her neck — they just stood and looked at one another. Jane watched the play of expressions across Dom's face. Delight, then thoughtfulness, then . . . desire. He leaned forward and kissed her again, lingeringly, softly. With a sigh, he took her by the hand and led her back to their towels. Jane remained in a sitting position while Dom lay on his back with his head in her lap. Automatically one of her hands went to his hair, still wet and mussed from their swim. She soon found that she was no longer just smoothing back the gleaming strands, but letting her cool fingers caress his scalp and forehead, his temples, his mouth.

"I love that," Dom said. "You have a magic touch. I could lie here like this for ever."

For ever. Oh, Jane thought, her heart

twisting, if only they had for ever. Instead they had only this moment. After tomorrow morning she might never see him again.

Almost as if reading her thoughts, Dom said softly, grasping her hand to still its movements, "Jane . . . "

"Yes?"

"I want to see you when I'm back in New York. Will you be there? For me, I mean?"

Jane's heart somersaulted. She tried to inject a lightness into her tone when she answered. "Of course. But do you really think you'll want to see me there, when you're back on your own turf, surrounded by all those glamor — "

Dom sat up abruptly and clapped on warm hand over her mouth. "Stop right there. Yes, I will want to see you." He scowled fiercely at her. "You got a problem with that, lady?"

"No, no," she cried. "I'll see you. I promise!"

His fake scowl changed to a genuine smile. Suddenly Jane was reminded of one small, or rather, tall, problem. Dom noted her tiny frown. "There is something wrong with my idea. Tell me."

"Well," she began slowly, "I know you're going to think this is silly, but, well, it's Deirdre."

Dom sat back and looked incredulously at her. "How on earth can Dee be a problem? Apart from her occasional pouts, she's great."

Jane looked at him sharply. "Pouts?"

"Well, hardy ever, actually. But today at the shoot she didn't seem very happy. Not quite her usual self. A little sulky, I guess you could say. But she's almost never like that. Anyway, it wasn't too hard for me to jolly her out of it. I thought maybe she was just feeling a little low after what happened to you yesterday and what with you leaving tomorrow and — "

"Oh, Dom," Jane said. "Shall I tell you why she was sulky today? She was furious that you and I were coming here together, just the two of us, this afternoon."

"Why should she be angry?"

Dom looked honestly puzzled and Jane felt like screaming in frustration. "Dom! Haven't you noticed that Deirdre has a wild crush on you? She takes every crumb you throw her and makes it into a wedding-cake. She thinks she's in love with you, and that you're just too 'cool' to admit you feel the same way. She thinks your asking her to go to Puerto Vallarta is an invitation to join her at the altar."

"Oh, come now," he said again. "She's not that stupid."

"She's not stupid at all, but she *is* that young!"

Dom looked uncertain. "I do tend to forget just how young Dee is. She looks so much older than fifteen and — " He ran a hand distractedly through his hair. "Oh, hell. I suppose I have been taking certain things for granted, just assuming she was old enough to understand."

Jane's expression turned bleak. "So, although I want to, um see you when we're all back in New York, I still have this problem with Deirdre. You should have heard her last night. She said she hates me. It was awful. And if she hates me for just today's outing, how is she going to react if we're seeing each other in New York? Dom — " Jane shook her head in despair "Deirdre thinks I'm stealing you from her. She believes you're in love with her. How can I convince her you're not? How?"

Dominic sat back on his heels and rubbed his thumb thoughtfully back and forth along his chin. "Look. Why don't I tell her? After all, it's me she's got the crush on, and she's going to believe it if I'm the one to tell her I'm not in love with her. I'll tell her when we're in Puerto Vallarta. I think I can convince her."

Jane looked at him gratefully. Yes, maybe this was the best way. "You're really quite a guy, you know. The other day, when we were watching the sunrise, you . . . you said that the man who rejected me was a fool. Well, so was Katya."

Dom reached up his hands to cup her face. "And you know what else? Another sure way I have of convincing Dee that I'm not in love with her?"

"What?" Jane breathed.

"I can tell her I'm in love with someone else."

Jane had her reservations about that idea, but maybe it'd help. "You'd better be prepared to supply her with a convincing name, though," she warned.

"No problem there at all," he said. "I really *am* in love with someone else. I wouldn't be making it up."

Jane's heart plummeted. So. He *was* just offering friendship. Affectionate friendship, perhaps, but that was all. She couldn't believe how devastated she felt. She didn't speak for a moment, and refused to meet Dom's gaze. At last she gathered herself together, curbed the sudden sting of tears behind her eyes and asked with false nonchalance,

"Who's the lucky lady?"

"You have to ask? Geez, you're making this hard for me," he said, shaking his head. "Jane, I'm in love with you. I didn't mean for this to happen, but there it is." He paused. "And, correct me if I'm wrong, Jane, but I think you're in love with me, too."

Such arrogance, Jane thought happily, dizzily. She poured herself into his arms, nuzzled her cheek into his warm neck. "Yes," she murmured. "I do love you."

Yes, she thought. Easy to love him, here on this deserted beach, in a foreign land, but back in New York where their lives were as different as the sun and the moon, where the photograph of his beautiful ex-wife adorned his living-room wall . . .

★ ★ ★

Back in her Cancun hotel room later that evening, Jane chastised herself for doubting him. He'd walked her to her door, kissed her good-night and again told her he loved her. Told her to believe him, trust him.

As she packed and got ready for bed, her thoughts swung to Deirdre. Just as she picked up the phone to call her room, there was a timid knock on her door.

It was Deirdre, standing there with a pleading look in her huge blue eyes.

"Oh, Jane," she began. "I'm so sorry about what I said last night. I didn't mean any of it. I didn't . . . "

Jane reached for her niece and gave her a hug. "I know you didn't, sweetie." She patted her back. "Everything's okay."

As she spoke, Jane thought that Deirdre, if she knew all that had taken place that day, would not think everything was okay. She prudently decided to say nothing. She wished Deirdre a wonderful trip to Puerto Vallarta, said she'd see her in four days, and that was that. Dom would take care of the rest.

Yet that night, her last night in Mexico, she lay awake for some time. She was going home to New York tomorrow morning. Dom was coming in another week. Deirdre would finally understand that her feelings for Dom were not returned. She would know that Dom was in love with her aunt. Katya wouldn't even play a part in all this. So what was her problem?

She rolled over and punched her pillow. Really, she was being silly.

11

"**W**OW. Guess Mexico agreed
with you."

"Hmm?"

"I said, Jane — " Nancy shook her
head in mock disgust, " — guess
Mexico agreed with you. I get the
feeling you're still there. If not in body,
then certainly in spirit."

"Oh, sorry, I — " Jane lifted her
gaze from the box of books she was
unpacking. "I, er, yes, had a nice
time."

Nice? Jane wanted to shout that
she'd had a wonderful, incredible time,
the most-important-time-of-her-life time,
but she couldn't. Not yet.

In the two years they had worked
together, Nancy had become a friend,
and Jane wanted to confide in her
— but not until she'd talked to Fred.
She owed him that. She had called

him on Sunday, the day after she had returned to New York. Her plan was to get together with him for dinner that very evening, give him the wallet she'd bought in Cancun as thanks for taking care of Seymour — and then tell him she wanted to end their relationship. And tell him why. It was a task she didn't relish, but it was only fair.

Yet when she'd called him he'd sounded strangely subdued. At her suggestion that they meet for dinner that same evening he'd muttered something about "kind of short notice, and I'm afraid I've made other plans . . . " Then, as if realizing his aloofness, he rushed on to make a date for the following evening.

And today, a van had pulled up outside the Book Nook, and its driver had hurried into the store with a bunch of flowers for a Miss Jane Cathcart. For a breathless moment Jane had thought they were from Dominic, but no. The little card accompanying the pretty yellow chrysanthemums said, *Welcome home. See you tonight. Fred.* When Jane remarked, "Funny. He usually sends roses," Nancy made no comment, which was also surprising.

Jane had fully anticipated — and, in the light of what she had to tell him, dreaded — a warm, enthusiastic welcome from Fred. He had always been so devoted to her. Maybe delivering her news would be a little easier.

Her thoughts swung to Sunday's other telephone conversation, which triggered a deep sigh of pleasure. The phone had rung at about nine in the evening, and Jane, in her bedroom reading, had snatched it up eagerly. As she'd hoped it had been Dom, just calling, he said, to see that she'd made it home safe and sound. He, Joss and Deirdre had flown to Puerto Vallarta on Sunday and had retired early, wanting to be rested for the shoot the next day.

Tentatively, Jane had asked him if he'd spoken to Deirdre.

There had been silence on the line

for a heartbeat, then Dom answered slowly, "The moment hasn't seemed right yet, Jane. Dee seems so elated right now, and I confess I'm worried about breaking her mood and ruining the shoot — "

"Look," Jane had said, "maybe you shouldn't speak to her. I'll do it when she gets back — "

"No, it's all right," Dom assured her. "I still think I'm the best one to break it to her. Forget what I said about Deirdre's possible bad mood. I think we can credit her with some maturity, some professionalism. She has to grow up sometime."

Jane sighed. "Yes, perhaps you're right."

"I think so. Not to worry, love. I'll find the right moment." Then he'd said disarmingly, "I watched the sun set this evening. God, I missed you."

"Oh, Dom," she'd answered softly. "I miss you, too. Terribly. I can't wait to see you! What day are you flying home? I'll meet you at the airport."

"No, don't do that," he'd replied. "It's Saturday, but I'll be with a whole entourage, and when I see you for the first time I want there to be just the two of us."

When at last they'd murmured their good-nights, Jane had lain awake for some time, her heart too full of love and longing and hope to permit sleep. The conversation had sent little jolts of excitement, and great shards of longing, through her. She'd felt a crazy flipflop in her midsection at the thought of the day they'd spent together on Isla Mujeres. When he'd taken her to the airport on Saturday morning before anyone else was up and around, her fears from the night before had been put to rest. She had been left with the wonderful certainty that she and Dom would be together soon, and he, somehow, would make everything all right with Deirdre, and all right with the world.

"So, are you seeing Fred tonight?" Nancy asked casually.

"Yes. He suggested we go to a new Italian place he's found."

"Oh, that'd be Enrico's on Thirty-Second."

"How do you know?" asked Jane, surprised.

Nancy was busy arranging the chrysanthemums. "Oh, I think Fred mentioned the place when he dropped by here last week . . ."

A woman over by the travel section was waving for attention. "Thanks, Nance," Jane said before she hurried over to help the woman. "You have a way with flowers. Anything green starts turning brown the moment I touch it."

"No problem," said Nancy, and Jane didn't stop to notice the look of misery on her assistant's face.

★ ★ ★

Fred blinked rapidly. "I . . . I was looking forward to seeing you, Jane, because there's something I want to

236

talk to you about."

"Oh," she said, taken aback. She'd thought she was the one who'd called this meeting. But maybe what Fred had to say would explain his decided lack of excitement about her return. "There's something I want to talk about with you, too." She paused and took note of the serious expression on his face. "Okay. You first."

"Well . . . " Fred put his fork down. "I'm sorry, Jane. I don't know how to say this."

What on earth . . . ? "Fred. It's all right. I'm your friend, remember?" Jane felt a surge of affection for him and knew that her claim was sincere. She smiled at him encouragingly. "Go on, Fred. It's all right," she repeated. "Really."

He took a deep breath, then plunged in. "I've begun seeing someone else."

That *was* startling news. She'd only been gone a week. But then, she reminded herself, look what had happened to her in a week. Why should she think it should be so different for everybody else?

"Oh, Fred," she said. "Don't look so stricken." To convince him that he hadn't plunged a knife into her heart, she added, "I've met someone, too. That's why I wanted to see you as soon as I got back. I wanted to tell you — "

Fred looked as startled as she had been. "Who? You met someone in Mexico?"

"Wait a minute, Fred. You first. Who are *you* seeing?" She found she was dying to know.

Fred looked a little sheepish, then replied, "Nancy."

Jane's mouth dropped open. "You're kidding!"

"Why should that surprise you?" Fred looked mildly annoyed, and Jane instantly apologized for her reaction.

Fred nodded. "I've known Nancy for a while. Not well, I grant you, but when you were away, and I stopped in the shop to ask her advice on what to do about a certain cat who refused to eat, she came with me to your place, coaxed that beast of yours into having supper, and then we went out and had a bite to eat ourselves. We got talking, I mean really talking, and one thing led to another, and . . . "

He shrugged helplessly. "Please don't get the wrong idea. We just found that we liked each other. Really liked each other. We've a lot in common, too. But neither Nancy nor I were about to betray you. We had to let you know about what was happening between us before we saw any more of each other, and so I said I'd tell you."

Jane recalled Nancy's odd behaviour in the shop earlier, and she smiled at him affectionately. "Oh, Fred, I'm happy for you and Nancy."

"So, who are you seeing?" Fred asked. "Who on earth did you meet in Mexico? Just because you and I aren't going to date any more doesn't mean I don't care about you."

The evening at the theatre when Fred

and Dom had met rose uncomfortably to mind. She took a deep breath. "Dom," she said. "Dominic Slater."

Fred sat back in his chair and blinked in astonishment. "You can't be serious, Jane. That guy's not for you. He'll only hurt you. He's a womanizer. Likes to be seen with gorgeous blondes dangling from his arm. I've seen the type — "

"No!" Jane nearly shouted. Lowering her voice self-consciously, she said, "No. You're wrong. I know him. He may seem like that, but he's not like that." Yet even as she spoke she knew Fred had voiced her own fears. She wasn't one of the beautiful ones. She wasn't Dominic's usual 'type'. But she was damned if she was going to let Fred know she harboured any insecurities.

Fred's brows drew together worriedly. "You know who you sound like? Your niece. What you're saying to me now is exactly what you told me *she* said about how she felt about this guy. For God's sake, Jane. I thought you knew better."

"Apparently I don't!" Jane snapped, then instantly regretted her outburst. Fred was just concerned, that was all. Softly she said, "I knew you'd think that, Fred, and that's one reason I dreaded telling you about him. About us. I know there's nothing I can say that'll convince you Dom's not a womanizer. I know he genuinely cares about me. Only time will show that to you, I imagine. But you'll see."

Fred's disapproval was still annoyingly evident as he reached across the table and placed his hand over hers. "I hope so, Jane. I really do."

★ ★ ★

"I knew it! The moment I saw him I knew he was the one for you!"

Edna Johnson slapped her latest historical-romance selection on the counter. *Depths of Desire*. Jane looked from the cover portrayal of the two slumbrous-eyed lovers to her grinning customer and said, "Who told you?

Sometimes I think I'll have to change the name of this store from the Book Nook to the Rumour Mill."

"It's not a rumour, is it, though?" declared Edna with a satisfied smile. "I saw you talking to that young man just before you went away. When I asked Nancy about him last week, she said he was in Mexico, too. Then she said that you two were an item now, or at least words to that effect, when I asked her."

"*Grilled* her, is more like it, Edna. I know you." Jane's tone was gently teasing, and she shook her untamed curls in a pretence of despair. "And now I suppose you're going to tell me that the girl on the cover of this book looks like me, too, aren't you?"

Edna chortled delightedly. "Well, yes, now that you mention it . . . "

"Oh, Edna, you are incorrigible."

"If you mean an incorrigible romantic, my dear, I take that as a compliment!"

At 6.30, Jane gathered her things to head back to her apartment. Deirdre, she knew, was coming home this evening, might in fact have already arrived. She suddenly felt a stab of anxiety. What frame of mind would her niece be in? Had Dom been able to let her down gently, make her realize that her love was only a silly infatuation? That she'd eventually, when she was older and ready, find love with the right man?

Had he told her about *them*?

When she opened the door to her apartment she nearly tripped over the suitcase that was standing just inside.

"Deirdre!" she called. She looked up from shoving the suitcase to one side and saw the girl curled up in a corner of the couch, her lustrous hair hanging partially over her face. Deirdre raised her head, and at first glance she looked fine. But her murmured hello said otherwise.

So did her red-rimmed eyes. Jane quickly crossed to her.

At her aunt's approach, Deirdre's demeanour changed dramatically from listlessness to abject misery. Great fat tears squeezed out of her eyes and began to roll down her cheeks.

"Deirdre, Deirdre, honey," Jane said, putting a comforting hand on her shoulder. "We didn't want to hurt you. It was just something that leapt up and took us both by surprise. Dominic and I found that . . . "

Her voice trailed off at the sudden look of genuine puzzlement on her niece's tear-streaked face. "What are you talking about, Aunt Jane? You and Dom . . . ?" Then Deirdre burst into hysterical laughter.

"What's so funny?" Jane asked, drawing back. "Didn't Dom tell you? He and I, well, he and I are in love."

Deirdre's face held a mixture of grief and pity. "Oh, Jane, he's done it to you, too."

"Done what, Deirdre? What are you talking about?" But even as she asked Jane's stomach wound into a knot of apprehension.

Deirdre leapt up from the couch and

began to pace the small living-room. "Katya," she said, throwing Jane a tormented look. "It's Katya he's in love with!"

Jane shook her head. "No, no, he's not. I know she was going to be in Puerto Vallarta, but he and his ex-wife are finished. He told me."

Deirdre stopped pacing and, with her hands wedged on her slim hips, faced Jane defiantly. "I saw them together, Jane. They are not 'finished', believe me."

"No!" Jane insisted. "Didn't Dom tell you? Didn't he say that he and I were — "

"He told me nothing! He *showed* me everything!"

"What do you mean?"

Deirdre collapsed dramatically on to the armchair. "He asked me to come have lunch with him in his room today after this morning's shoot. He said he wanted to have a talk with me, and then he'd see that I got a cab to the airport. When I got to his room the door was open a little, so I just walked in and — "

"For God's sake, Deirdre, what? Go on!"

"They were kissing, Jane." When her aunt said nothing, she embellished, "Katya and Dom were kissing like . . . lovers! I walked right in in the middle of it, and . . . when Dom saw me he looked furious. I was just so flabbergasted, I turned and ran out of there. I was already packed, so I just grabbed my bags from my room, got a cab and went to the airport. It was obvious to me that Dom and Katya didn't need to be interrupted. You were right, Aunt Jane. I really was an idiot to think he loved me. And now you . . . "

Jane closed her eyes and took a moment to collect her thoughts. She had to make some sense out of this. There had to be a reasonable explanation.

Two came to mind.

One was that this was the way he'd

chosen to let Deirdre know he didn't love her. Finding the object of her infatuation wrapped in the arms of another woman had certainly given her the message. Perhaps more effectively than any other way.

But that was so mean, so cruel. Cowardly. How could she love a man like that?

The second possible explanation was no better for Jane's peace of mind. It meant that Dom's words of love were as temporary as the click of a shutter. He didn't really love her, Jane, at all.

Any way you shook it and let it settle, the residue was the same. She and Dom were finished. Finished, she thought with a ghastly lurch of her innards, before they'd really got started. Oh, yes, they'd exchanged passionate kisses and words of love, but what did that mean? It had been far away, in another world, almost in another time. And the man in question had neither the desire nor the need to curtail his lust, or love, or whatever it was he felt for his ex-wife, out of any sort of loyalty to a naive, unsophisticated, pretty-but-not-beautiful woman who had briefly, oh so briefly, taken his fancy.

As she lay in bed that night, Seymour traitorously purring contentedly at her feet, she wondered what she would say to Dom when he called her again from Puerto Vallarta. *If* he called, she amended. For suddenly the picture was clear to her. He would be too busy all right. Too busy watching sunsets with the beautiful Katya. Too busy making love to her.

Her hurt changed to anger. The rat! she thought. He was not a caring man, as she'd so firmly assured Fred. He was a monster. He must be. For why hadn't he called her tonight, especially in the light of what Deirdre had seen today? Wouldn't he want to explain?

There was only one reason for his not calling, she realized. Because he didn't really care for her. Jane felt as if she'd been kicked in the stomach. When he called, *if* he called, she'd snarl a thanks at him for getting the message to her niece, then hang up the phone in his arrogant ear.

She flipped her sleep-defying body on to its other side, hoping that her newfound determination would give her some peace. It did not.

★ ★ ★

No call came from Mexico all week, which only confirmed Jane's opinion that Dom was a scoundrel. She'd been taken in. Thank heaven she hadn't let things go too far with him when she was in Mexico.

On Saturday morning there was a surprising delivery for Jane at the shop. A single red rose, with the note: *Be with you, my love, before the sun sets.*

Jane looked at the scarlet bloom and the words incredulously. Did Dom really think she awaited his return like Isolde awaiting her Tristan? She felt like tearing the petals off the rose and tossing them into the trash.

She had decided to tell no one what Deirdre had said, nor talk about her own dismal realization that Fred had been right about Dominic. The humiliation was too much. For the rest of the day, her thoughts swung constantly to how she was going to avoid seeing or talking to Dom. It wasn't going to be easy. The rose he'd sent showed that he had every intention of calling her when he was home. He'd no doubt phone her the minute she was back in her apartment after work. Her best defence was offence, she decided. She would not let him know how hurt she was, how damaged her pride. She would not be made a fool of.

The phone was ringing as she walked in the door. Deirdre was nowhere in sight, so Jane steeled herself and picked up the receiver.

"Jane, I'm back! I've got to see you. Grab a cab and come over here," Dom's voice rumbled in her ear. "I've got a bottle of wine on ice, the glasses are chilling, and the steaks are ready to go. We'll have dinner, then — "

"No."

"Pardon? Jane, are you all right? Come on, sweetheart, I can't wait to see you. Do you need a little time to get ready?" He chuckled. "You know I won't care how you look, you don't have to wash your hair, do your nails, or — "

"Dominic," Jane interrupted coldly, "I'm not coming over." She paused and was strangely satisfied to hear Dom's sharp intake of air. "I . . . I can't see you anymore. It was a mistake." She rushed on, bolder now. "I thought I loved you, but I don't. It was just one of those holiday things." She gave a brittle little laugh. "I'm not sure what came over me, but it's gone now. I can't believe you feel any different about it than I do. Once you've been in New York a few days, you'll see. I'm sure you understand."

There was a long moment of silence at the other end of the line, then Dom said harshly, "Yes, I guess I do." The phone clicked in her ear.

As Jane replaced the receiver, tears were starting to form in her eyes. She blinked them away impatiently, thinking, It's better this way. Cleaner, simpler. Her pride was still intact. What use was there in going into her reasons? They were like beings from two different planets. They didn't speak the same language.

But when she went to bed that night she kept hearing his voice saying as they watched the sun rise, "Now we'll never be lonely again . . . "

12

SEPTEMBER was as unseasonably chilly as August had been warm. Business at the Book Nook was brisk, Deirdre was back in school in Dubuque, and Seymour was his usual demanding self. In mid-month, Jane received a flower-embossed note from her niece thanking her for everything, telling her that school was a 'real drag' after New York, but there was this new guy in her class, a 'real hunk' ... She didn't say a word about Dominic Slater.

Dominic. She'd thought she could live with the knowledge that, despite what had happened between them in Mexico, he wasn't right for her, and she wasn't right for him. He was part of that world of beautiful, larger-than-life people, a world that had nothing to do with her.

But as the weeks passed, Jane was no closer to finding some sort of peace. On a Monday morning in the middle of the month, Jane answered the phone in the Book Hook with her usual briskness.

"Is that you, Jane?"

She instantly recognized Joss's voice. There was a moment's silence, then Joss said, "Jane, please don't think I'm just being an interfering old woman. But I feel I must talk to you. Could we meet for a drink?"

Jane's heart had begun to beat erratically. "All right."

"How about tonight? About seven? I can come to the Village . . . "

In the end they arranged to meet in a quiet little pub not far from the Book Nook. When Jane walked into the place she spotted Joss's beautifully coiffed silver hair right away. The woman was sitting nursing a drink at a small table by the wall. She spotted Jane at about the same time and lifted a hand in greeting.

"Thank you for coming," were Joss's

first words. "I wasn't sure you would."

Jane was surprised. "Why would you think that?"

Joss snorted. "Well, you have been rather scarce this past month."

"That's because I — " Jane stopped. What could she say?

"Because . . . ?" Joss quirked an eyebrow. "Yes. That's why I wanted to see you. I wanted to find out what in God's name happened between you two."

Jane was taken aback. She tried to sound nonchalant. "Oh, it was just one of those things."

Joss suddenly looked fierce. "One of what things? Jane, I wanted to talk to you because Dom is an absolute wreck. And he's become a royal pain in the you-know-what to work with. Even the models notice it."

She paused and studied Jane. "Speaking of wrecks, if you don't mind my saying, I've seen you look better."

Jane was thinner. And the fact that

she hadn't been sleeping well was evidenced by her lustreless hair and the little mauve smudges under her eyes. Remembering Joss's habit of speaking her mind, she didn't take offence at the comment. "Well, I guess I've been working too-long hours lately."

"I suspect that's not really the problem," Joss snapped. "I think you're suffering from the same thing as Dom."

"What's that?" Jane asked.

"Lovesickness. A broken heart. A lovers' spat. I don't know. You tell me. I only know that ever since we got back to New York in August, he hasn't been the same man. He told me all about you two, so of course I expected to see you around when we were back. But then, poof!" Joss snapped her fingers. "You'd vanished."

Jane was still determined to hang on to her pride. "Come on. You seem to think Dom and I had something going. Well, we didn't. It was just one of those holiday things."

"Nonsense!" declared Joss. "It was a lot more than that. Don't you pretend otherwise."

Jane felt her eyes fill with tears. "Yes, yes, it was. But only to me, Joss. Don't you see? To Dom, it was nothing." She couldn't tell Joss about what Deirdre had seen. "He can have any woman he wants. They're around him all the time — "

"You're wrong, Jane. Do one thing." Joss reached over, and grasped Jane's hand. "Go see him. Talk to him."

★ ★ ★

The brass lion head seemed to taunt her. Jane stared at it and refused to be intimidated. If nothing else was accomplished, she could at least get things off her chest. Exorcise whatever demons were robbing her of her sleep.

She reached up, gripped the knocker and banged it. Hard.

Dom answered her knock. The first thing Jane noticed was that he seemed thinner, his face lined, even haggard. As he took in the dark-clad, tousled-haired figure standing on his stoop, his expression changed rapidly from impatience to surprise to anger. His blue eyes turned wintry. "So it's you," he said. "What are you doing here?"

He didn't stand aside, made no move to show that Jane could enter. Undaunted, she asked, "May I come in? I — I have to talk to you."

He seemed irresolute for a moment, then with a weary sigh, he stepped aside and gestured for her to enter. "Sure, why not?" He waved an arm toward the small anteroom, and Jane moved forward, brushing against him as she did so. She was appalled at the way the brief contact sent a shock wave through her system.

"Take your coat off," he suggested when he followed her inside.

"No," said Jane stiffly. "I won't be staying long." The truth was, despite the warmth of the room, Jane felt chilled.

"So," he said when she hesitated, "what did you have to tell me?"

Jane was lost for a moment. Exactly what *did* she want to say? Suddenly she wished she hadn't come.

"Oh, do come on, Jane. Speak." He cocked his head to one side. "Hmm. Let me guess. Did you come here to apologize for your rudeness when I got back from Mexico and was expecting some sort of, er, pleasant welcome?" He gave a short bark of laughter. "A bit late for that, my dear. Or is it that you've misplaced your niece again?"

Jane straightened her shoulders. "Yes, no. I mean, I want to talk about my niece, yes, but she's not missing. She's at home now, in Iowa."

"Phew. That's a relief. I really wasn't looking forward to seeing more male strippers."

Jane blushed at his reference, then snapped, "All right. There is one thing I've wanted to know. How could you tell her in that way? How could you be so callous?"

Dominic looked perplexed. "Tell who in what way? How was I callous?"

Jane rounded on him, angry now. "You know very well what I'm talking about. I'm talking about the way you let Deirdre know you didn't love her."

"Ah," he exclaimed. "Look. I didn't *tell* Dee anything. I meant to, I really did, but she was gone before I had the chance. I wanted to call you, but I never got a chance to do that, either."

Jane was amazed that he would give her such a feeble excuse, and her feelings showed on her face.

"Look," he said, "I don't care if you believe me or not, but we were incredibly busy that week. Our shoots went on until practically ten o'clock every night, because the client wanted the effect of the night sky. And what with the two-hour time difference I was never back at the hotel before 1 a.m. New York time. We were never anywhere near a phone during the day, so I couldn't even call you at your shop. Besides, I knew — " his face twisted cynically — "I'd be seeing you at the end of the week, so I thought it didn't really matter."

Jane couldn't contain herself any longer. "No," she snapped. "It didn't really matter. All that really mattered to you was Katya!"

A light dawned in his eyes. "So *that* was your problem." He gave a self-satisfied smile that made Jane want to smack him. She resisted the urge as he continued, "But you, knew Katya was going to be there. You knew — "

Jane lost it then, and she rounded on him furiously. "Yes, I knew she would be there. But I didn't know that you two would be going at it like a pair of animals in heat!"

"Very prettily put, Jane."

Her face flushed a deep red and she mumbled, "Sorry. I had no right to say that."

His shoulders slumped. "I gather Dee told you about walking into my room when Katya was there?"

"Of course, but hey, it's your life. I've no right — " She stopped, unable to keep up a cool front. "Look, I just want to say that it was a rather unkind way for Deirdre to get the message about how you felt about her." And, Jane thought, an awful way for her to get the same message.

Dominic looked astounded. "Is that what you think? You think I set up that little scene just to illustrate my point to Dee? What kind of a guy do you think I am? Tell me, Jane." Dominic's eyes blazed. "Come on, tell me that you think I'm capable of any sort of cruelty to achieve my selfish ends. Tell me . . . "

To her horror, Jane started to cry. She quickly turned her back to him and wiped furiously at her tears.

Dominic closed the gap between them in two swift strides. Reaching out, he grasped her shoulder and twisted her around to face him. She kept her head lowered.

"Look at me," he said, his voice

suddenly gentle. When she refused to do so, stubbornly keeping her gaze fixed on the pearl-grey carpet, he slowly put a finger under her chin and lifted it. "You're crying," he said. "Why?"

"I'm not!" Jane protested.

"Then what is that?" Dominic asked, tracing the watery path etched by a tear on her cheek.

At his tenderness, tears welled up even more thickly in her eyes. Dominic moved quickly and in less than a second, she was in his arms. "Jane, Jane, my little love. Forgive me, please. I never wanted to hurt you."

He held her tighter, as if his very closeness could convince her of the sincerity of his words. Jane clung to him like a drowning woman, as if her life depended on his strength.

"Shh," he said, as her crying ebbed. Then he stepped back slightly and with his hands cradling her damp face, said, "I wanted to tell Dee about us, about you and me, that day, before she got on the plane. I told her to come to my room — I thought we'd talk there. My dear ex — " Dom sighed heavily " — chose that moment to pay me a visit. She said she'd come to realize our break-up was a mistake. She was sure I'd forgive her and take her back. I started to tell her that there was no chance of our ever getting back together when she decided to try to convince me in a more, er, physical way."

He shook his head wearily. "That's when Dee made her entrance. She thought she was seeing me kissing Katya, but it was the other way around. Katya was kissing me. It was a desperate attempt to get the response she wanted. There was a time," he admitted, "when Katya could just touch me and I was hers. Sometimes we'd fight, but she had only to apologize, start kissing me, and I'd be in love all over again. But she lost that power over me a long time ago."

Jane tipped her head back and

anchored her gaze to his. "I can't believe that. Katya is so incredibly beautiful! No man can resist her."

Dom grabbed her hand. "Come with me."

Puzzled, Jane let him lead her up the stairs to his apartment. Still gripping her hand he pulled her close to one of the picture-covered walls. It was the same wall that had held the exquisite photograph of Katya in an English garden. Jane didn't want to see it again, and she kept her gaze lowered.

"Look, Jane," Dom commanded. "Lift that stubborn head of yours and look!"

Recognizing the pointlessness of defying him, Jane did as he instructed.

What she saw on the wall took her breath away.

It was a large colour photo of a woman leaning against a crumbling stone pillar. The expression on her face was illusive, indefinable, yet compelling. Her full lips were slightly parted, her cheeks were a soft pink, her hair was a lustrous dark tumble about her face. She was beautiful.

"It's me," Jane murmured wonderingly. She turned questioningly to Dom. "I can't quite believe it. You've touched it up. You've — "

"No." His voice was almost harsh. "No, Jane. That is you. And you — " he paused, closing his eyes briefly " — are beautiful."

Jane looked again at the lovely framed photograph. "But I'm not one of your models. Why did you put it on your wall?"

He smiled. "I put the work I'm most proud of on my walls, Jane." Then he took her hand once more and pulled her down the hallway and into his bedroom.

He picked up a small gilt-framed photo from the table beside the bed. "I like to put my favourite photographs in my living-room. I like to put a picture of the woman I love here." He showed the photograph to Jane, and this time she immediately recognized

266

it as another of the ones he took of her in Tulum.

She turned her gaze to him and stood quietly while he put his hand to her hair and tenderly, oh so tenderly, drew on a curl. "I put the picture here, Jane, so that her face is the first thing I see in the morning when I wake up, and the last thing I see before I go to sleep at night."

Jane continued to stand, unmoving, while his hand moved from her hair on to her cheek, and from there, down her neck, and over one shoulder. Softly he said, "Do you see now? Do you understand what you mean to me? How I've waited for the day you would come back?"

She grasped his hand with her own and held it to her as if it were the most precious thing in the world. And at that moment it was. *He* was. Eyes liquid with emotion, she whispered, "I understand now. I'm sorry — "

He pulled her gently into his arms. "No. You don't have to be sorry. You just have to say — " a tiny pause "you love me the way I love you."

Happiness sang through Jane. "I do! I do love you, love you, love you . . . "
Her words were stopped only when his head bent and his lips covered hers.

★ ★ ★

The following headline and story ran under a photograph in the social column of a mid-November edition of *The Dubuque Chronicle*:

PICTURE PERFECT

Dubuque native Jane Cathcart and her fiancé, New York fashion photographer Dominic Slater, were all smiles as they descended the steps of St Barnabas Church after their wedding Saturday afternoon. The matron of honour was Sharon Flaherty of Dubuque, the bride's older sister. The bridesmaids were

Deirdre Flaherty, the bride's niece, who has put her modelling career on hold while she finishes her schooling, and Nancy Barstow, a friend of Miss Cathcart's from New York City, where the bride has lived and worked for the past six years. Miss Cathcart was given away by William Flaherty, her brother-in-law. Also in attendance were Mrs Joss Alvino and Fred Anderson, Miss Barstow's fiancé, also of New York. The newly-weds will be spending their honeymoon in Hawaii, where 'the sun rises and sets like no other place in the world', said the handsome groom. The couple plan to reside in Manhattan, where the bride owns and operates a successful bookshop, and the groom will continue his renowned career in fashion photography. When asked what brought them together, Miss Cathcart said, 'My niece, Deirdre, and a sunrise in Tulum.' Mr Slater added enigmatically, 'We had a little

help from my Aunt Bethesda, too.'
Whatever the cause, the result is one
very happy couple. Don't they make
a perfect pair?

THE END

WITH SOMEBODY ELSE
Theresa Charles

Rosamond sets off for Cornwall with Hugo to meet his family, blissfully unaware of the shocks in store for her.

A SUMMER FOR STRANGERS
Claire Hamilton

Because she had lost her job, her flat and she had no money, Tabitha agreed to pose as Adam's future wife although she believed the scheme to be deceitful and cruel.

VILLA OF SINGING WATER
Angela Petron

The disquieting incidents that occurred at the Vatican and the Colosseum did not trouble Jan at first, but then they became increasingly unpleasant and alarming.

DOCTOR NAPIER'S NURSE
Pauline Ash

When cousins Midge and Derry are entered as probationer nurses on the same day but at different hospitals they agree to exchange identities.

A GIRL LIKE JULIE
Louise Ellis

Caroline absolutely adored Hugh Barrington, but then Julie Crane came into their lives. Julie was the kind of girl who attracts men without even trying.

COUNTRY DOCTOR
Paula Lindsay

When Evan Richmond bought a practice in a remote country village he did not realise that a casual encounter would lead to the loss of his heart.

ENCORE
Helga Moray

Craig and Janet realise that their true happiness lies with each other, but it is only under traumatic circumstances that they can be reunited.

NICOLETTE
Ivy Preston

When Grant Alston came back into her life, Nicolette was faced with a dilemma. Should she follow the path of duty or the path of love?

THE GOLDEN PUMA
Margaret Way

Catherine's time was spent looking after her father's Queensland farm. But what life was there without David, who wasn't interested in her?

HOSPITAL BY THE LAKE
Anne Durham

Nurse Marguerite Ingleby was always ready to become personally involved with her patients, to the despair of Brian Field, the Senior Surgical Registrar, who loved her.

VALLEY OF CONFLICT
David Farrell

Isolated in a hostel in the French Alps, Ann Russell sees her fiancé being seduced by a young girl. Then comes the avalanche that imperils their lives.

NURSE'S CHOICE
Peggy Gaddis

A proposal of marriage from the incredibly handsome and wealthy Reagan was enough to upset any girl — and Brooke Martin was no exception.

A DANGEROUS MAN
Anne Goring

Photographer Polly Burton was on safari in Mombasa when she met enigmatic Leon Hammond. But unpredictability was the name of the game where Leon was concerned.

PRECIOUS INHERITANCE
Joan Moules

Karen's new life working for an authoress took her from Sussex to a foreign airstrip and a kidnapping; to a real life adventure as gripping as any in the books she typed.

VISION OF LOVE
Grace Richmond

When Kathy takes over the rundown country kennels she finds Alec Stinton, a local vet, very helpful. But their friendship arouses bitter jealousy and a tragedy seems inevitable.

CRUSADING NURSE
Jane Converse

It was handsome Dr. Corbett who opened Nurse Susan Leighton's eyes and who set her off on a lonely crusade against some powerful enemies and a shattering struggle against the man she loved.

WILD ENCHANTMENT
Christina Green

Rowan's agreeable new boss had a dream of creating a famous perfume using her precious Silverstar, but Rowan's plans were very different.

DESERT ROMANCE
Irene Ord

Sally agrees to take her sister Pam's place as La Chartreuse the dancer, but she finds out there is more to it than dyeing her hair red and looking like her sister.

HEART OF ICE
Marie Sidney

How was January to know that not only would the warmth of the Swiss people thaw out her frozen heart, but that she too would play her part in helping someone to live again?

LUCKY IN LOVE
Margaret Wood

Companion-secretary to wealthy gambler Laura Duxford, who lived in Monaco, seemed to Melanie a fabulous job. Especially as Melanie had already lost her heart to Laura's son, Julian.

NURSE TO PRINCESS JASMINE
Lilian Woodward

Nick's surgeon brother, Tom, performs an operation on an Arabian princess, and she invites Tom, Nick and his fiancé to Omander, where a web of deceit and intrigue closes about them.

THE WAYWARD HEART
Eileen Barry

Disaster-prone Katherine's nickname was "Kate Calamity", but her boss went too far with an outrageous proposal, which because of her latest disaster, she could not refuse.

FOUR WEEKS IN WINTER
Jane Donnelly

Tessa wasn't looking forward to meeting Paul Mellor again — she had made a fool of herself over him once before. But was Orme Jared's solution to her problem likely to be the right one?

SURGERY BY THE SEA
Sheila Douglas

Medical student Meg hadn't really wanted to go and work with a G.P. on the Welsh coast although the job had its compensations. But Owen Roberts was certainly not one of them!

HEAVEN IS HIGH
Anne Hampson

The new heir to the Manor of Marbeck had been found. But it was rather unfortunate that when he arrived unexpectedly he found an uninvited guest, complete with stetson and high boots.

LOVE WILL COME
Sarah Devon

June Baker's boss was not really her idea of her ideal man, but when she went from third typist to boss's secretary overnight she began to change her mind.

ESCAPE TO ROMANCE
Kay Winchester

Oliver and Jean first met on Swale Island. They were both trying to begin their lives afresh, but neither had bargained for complications from the past.